Ayesha Muzaffar

JINNISTAN

Scary stories to tell over chai.

Published by Liberty Publishing
C–16, Sector 31–A Mehran Town Extension,
Korangi Industrial Area, Karachi – Pakistan
www.libertybooks.com

This edition first being published in Pakistan

1 2 3 4 5 6 7 8 9 10

This is a work of fiction. Names, characters, places and incidents are either the product of the author's imagination or are used fictitiously or any resemblance to any actual person; living or dead, events or locales are entirely coincidental.

ISBN: 978–969–8729–240

For abu jaan, Malik Muzaffar, a man whose cotton shawl leaves the scent of bravery, he who taught me that life is nothing but a kebab and should be lived one bite at a time,
For ama jaan, Sanila Muzaffar, my best friend and the woman who taught me the difference between *kay* and *keh* in Urdu for ten years,
For nano jaan, my second mother,
For my late dada abu, the man Sharaqpur recognizes,
For Farhan, for letting me be the *sheera* to his gulabjamun,
For 119 E, the welcoming roof under which I wrote these tales,
For Salma, my Moroccan friend
For Sugar Courted, for catering to my *meetha* cravings,
For Momina and Hajera, the two princesses without whom none of this would have been possible,
For Iqra, Sa*jee*r and Nibhaan,
You are all a part of this.

Chapter 1

3 Men 3 Stories

The grains of Karachi's muddy sand feel like home as they slide between Yawar's toes. He often comes to the beach after Maghrib time, when the cool summer–time breeze has replaced the scent of camels and their urine; when the colorful clothing of women with wailing children hanging on their waists has been replaced by a clearer, calmer, and colorless view of the night.

Cities apart, Mehmood rubs his beard and orders a diet Pepsi with his medium–rare beef steak and baked potatoes. He dips his finger into the hummus sauce and plays with it. The texture is gritty, and his frown makes it obvious that he likes his dips smoother, just like his ami used to make them. His second wife, sitting across him, sighs. All she has ever wanted in life was a man's undivided attention and bhaiyya's kebabs for lunch, and today, she has none.

Sandwiched between Lahore and Karachi, in the city of *darbars* and sohan halwa, Naveed sits in front of his autistic son, visually explaining the shapes of clouds, waiting for him to chuckle every time he waves his hands in a circular motion. "Biryani!" says his son. *"Nahin,"* replies Naveed. "Clouds. Badal, *betay.* Badal."

"Biryani!" giggles his son.

This is the story of three men; three men with different lives, different solutions, but the same problem–jinns.

❶

Yawar wasn't always like this; he didn't skip family dinners with aunty Parveen's *khandaan* to enjoy a quiet night at the beach by himself. As far as Yawar could recall, he never liked the beach–at least not till some months ago.

Aunty Parveen did not mind. Yawar had been in her *nazar* for the longest time, and she was utterly delighted to have him engaged to her daughter, Mahzaeb. Mahzaeb, too, was on cloud nine knowing that she'd be getting married to the cousin everyone had secretly wanted to get hitched to. She had never talked directly to Yawar because she felt that it was her shyness that he very much approved of, *warna* the other cousins were bold and *nangi pungi.*

It was true that Yawar was not inclined towards his other cousins, but it was also true that he had no interest in Mahzaeb. It wasn't because they had grown up calling each other *bhai bhen,* but because Yawar felt that he was already married.

Yawar had always been interested in physics and its laws. He explained life through that particular science, and he believed that nothing fell outside its numerical boundaries. So, when his dadi ama claimed to talk to jinns, he laughed. He sat massaging the tips of her wrinkled, *khajoor*–like feet, and heard stories about how a jinn lived in his dado's room. On one occasion, he was explicitly told not to play with his Bob the Builder toy truck in the corner of the room because the jinn lived there. When dadi ama wasn't home, Yawar sat in that corner and played there for hours.

He witnessed something very fascinating; when he rolled the truck towards the corner, it sped sideways, like somebody was throwing it away. After the truck would land on its top, Yawar would examine its tires. Almost always, they were burning hot. So, Yawar took it upon himself to study that corner. After analyzing it for days, Yawar came across a faulty wire that had been let loose behind the curtains; because of the current passing through it, it charged anything metallic thrown its way. And so, the young man concluded that his dadi's jinn was, in fact, roaming electricity.

When Yawar was at NUST, his professor relayed an account he had with an energy disguised as a human and told the class that jinns were actually energy, and that they very much existed. Yawar guffawed. He told sir Suleman that he was mistaken, for energies were anything but human, and jinns they certainly were not. He wrote his thesis on how kinetic energy could turn into sound energy and motion energy, and finally, any energy the brain perceived, but it was not anything supernatural. To Yawar, what could not yet be explained by science would be put into the realms of parapsychology, for it was the easiest alternative, one that did not require hard work.

One night, when Yawar's mama, ami Najma, congratulated the family on her son's *baat paki* ceremony, Yawar crept outside. The roads were closed due to Imran Khan's protests, and due to a container blocking the entrance of the main road, he ended up at the beach in the middle of the night. There was a couple there, holding hands, very much in love, and Yawar rolled his eyes. To him, love was like jinn – explainable by science. Perhaps it was a chemical reaction – the same kind as the dopamine rush he felt when studying nuclear fission – that people termed 'love'.

In an hour, the voices outside had reduced to indistinct murmurs, the couple had left, and Yawar stood in the farthest corner of the beach, examining the water circle around his toes. A honk–like sound disrupted his thoughts, and he examined the roaring waves through a bird's eye view. *Honk.* There it was again, louder this time. After five long minutes, Yawar saw a wooden boat wash up on the shore a little distance away.

It's the middle of the night. The waves are ruthless. How have they spared this boat and its owner? Yawar contemplated as he ran towards the boat. Upon reaching it, he saw a woman lying inside, her figure now loosely hugged by the moist sand. The woman appeared to be ill, for she lay lifelessly on the wooden plank. Her face was covered by a thick layer of silky, straight hair that shone under the October moonlight.

"Suniye?" Yawar blurted out. He didn't know what to *say*. A part of him was Thinking about the hon*ki*ng sound; there was no machinery on the wooden boat. The other part wanted to wake the woman up, but he concluded that she might be dead and that he could get in trouble. He had seen enough CID to know better.

"Suniye jee," he repeated with more gusto. Yawar rocked the boat. Well, at least he tried roc*ki*ng it. The weight of the petite woman was heavier than the gigantic bottle of Nestlé that his ama made him place on the dispenser. Ever since he was a child, Yawar had always thought a lot, which was his most pressing problem. As a young boy, he'd calculate the pros and cons of consuming the grape ice–lolly, and the orange one.

He thought about running away from the scene, but then he thought that abandoning the lady would be inhumane. He thought a lot. "Hello, *jee?*"

Yawar placed his hand on the woman's head. Her hair was drenched, and she was cold. He took off his jacket and placed it on top of her. Yawar sat there, looking at the moon and then his jacket, and then at the moon again.

Slowly, he slid the jacket enough to catch a glimpse of

her face, now that the moon hung right above them. He then brushed the hair off her face using the back of his hand.

Yawar gulped. The lady was unlike any woman he had seen before, and as a child, he had seen many Bollywood movies with ama; none of the women had appealed to him. Her radiant face appeared to be lit up like a lamp. Her features weren't South Asian. The nose was round, and her tiny lips painted the color of *anaar* were covered in water drops. He wondered if she was Chinese or Japanese. Her face was too oval to be Korean.

"Excuse me?" he said. The nervousness made Yawar's toes tickle. He placed his hand on her cheek, banishing the patches of dirt from the beauty tantamount to the brightest in a *ki*ngdom of stars. *A star. Sitara–that's what she is, he wondered.*

Yawar sat there, peacefully, *chaunkri maar kay.* He smiled to himself and waited. He waited for what seemed like an hour that drudged by as slowly and laboriously as the boat. And then, he saw the lady fidget. At that exact time, his phone started to vibrate.

Yawar quickly declined the call. It was not him being disrespectful; it was just that the lady in front of him lay so peacefully that he did not want to wake her up this way. So, he decided that his ama could wait.

The woman was young, though deciphering even her roundabout age would be a challenge–her face was too ethnically ambiguous. Her small, sea-green eyes followed

Yawar's the moment she opened them. At once, the silence between them gave Yawar immense pleasure, as if looking into her eyes had been his life–long dream. She collected herself ever so gently, like the owner of a precious necklace does when it breaks, and the beads scatter across the floor. It was when she lifted her upper body from the floor that Yawar noticed her feet were twisted–turned backwards–and yet, he thought that those, too, were indeed beautiful.

"Hello. My name is Yawar. I–I saw that you had–" Yawar spoke in his finest accent, the language of *angraez,* for he was sure that they did not share their descent, and the little clothing she wore suggested that she hadn't been nestled in Pakistan either.

"Adaab." She opened her mouth, and words just flew out of it, like Lahori car drivers running across each other, in four different directions, instinctively aware of the way. *"Adaab,* Yawar *Sahab."*

She knew Yawar's name, and she smiled when she said it. Her little lips parted, and deep–set, even little dimples formed under both her cheeks, running perpendicular to her laugh lines. She was an early birthday present.

And so, that night, under the stars and the tranquility of the sky, Yawar and the girl conversed for hours. She told him that she wasn't human and that he ought to be afraid–but Yawar wasn't. She told him that she was what he might call a siren–*been wali aurat,* an entity that his chapters could not explain. Yawar liked how straightforward she was, how there was no small talk or brushing over the edges between them. Everything was out on the table, and not once did he question how she knew so much about him. He just sat there, listening to her tell him tales of sinking ships, leading captains astray, seducing men to surrender their body to ruthless waves, and how well she could sing.

She sang. She honked. Yawar watched in amusement. She could sound like the wind, like his abba's downtrodden car–but most beautifully. She could sound like the sizzling sound of his phupho's poori from the previous night being reheated on the stove, and even like his phupho herself. She was a star–a *sitara.*

She told him that she could kill him, that just like the *dayans* living on the land, she was a *makhlook* of God, and she could very much kill him.

Yawar had mild urges to *say Bismillah.* He knew the *kalmas.* But he didn't want her to leave, and she, the cunning, gorgeous creature of the sea, could sense it.

And so, they both made love. And she whispered in his ear that on the Day of Judgment, he'd burn in the deepest depths of hell if he did so, but Yawar engaged. He had never felt such a connection before. Mesmerized by her beauty, Yawar did not measure his doings by science and its facts for the first time in his life.

Yawar returned home with the biggest grin plastered across his face at Fajar time. He could see men crowding in the masjid and the occurrence of the prayer, but he could not hear the words of God. He tried to. He went inside and told them all to speak louder, but his ears had become deaf to the sayings of the Lord.

And now, married to Mahzaeb, Yawar often sits at the farthest corner of the beach, waiting for a boat to wash up against the shore. He does so, not to make love to the maiden, but because it has been twelve years since he last heard a holy recitation, and pus oozes out of his starved–out ear canals every time he strains too hard in attempts to listen.

Mehmood loved Bibi Bakhtawar. He loved how she made the perfect square *parathas,* and how she always forgot to send him lunch at his shop in Liberty market. He loved how she tried out the entire stock at Khaadi before buying a single *shalwar* to go with an old suit. He loved how she drooled on her pillow at night. He loved her double chin, and that one hair that grew out of the mole under her cheek. He loved how when his bhabi went for facials, Bakhtawar stayed home and applied *ubtan,* because she believed in Zubaida apa *kay totkay.* Mehmood loved her. Bakhtawar was his *jaan.* And so, when she died during childbirth on a hot summer afternoon, Mehmood was devastated.

They had a baby girl. Mehmood and his Bakhto. They hadn't known the gender before, and both of them had wanted a *nanni pari*. Mehmood held the child in his arms and wept. She looked just like his Bakhto. The resemblance was uncanny, because of which from that day onwards, Mehmood found it near impossible to look at his daughter. Mehmood was a good man; he believed that he was, and so, he remarried within a month–not because he wanted to, but because little Saniya needed a mother.

Nagma and Mehmood shared no intimacy, and Mehmood had made clear to her that there was a possibility that he would never love her. But the house was hers, and all his money was hers, and he would never cheat on her. He could never come to love her. At first, Nagma thought that looking after Saniya would help win Mehmood over, but it didn't, and neither did getting dolled up with her *jhumkas.* Her dadi's traditional *chaawal* recipe that had been fool–proof at winning over husbands' affections since her great grandmother's time did not work either.

Mehmood occasionally took Nagma and Saniya to dinners. He loved food, and then again, he was a good man. Years passed, and Nagma grew fond of Saniya. Her little toes grew into big ones, and she started to walk and run; her chuckles turned into *mama naja,* and her straight, silky hair curled up into short waves. And at the end of the day, it seemed it was only Nagma and Saniya, and their happiness.

When Saniya turned nine, Mehmood took up a project–based job and left for Gujrat. At night, when Saniya missed her papa, not knowing what real fathers were like, she wept. Their house was out of Slanty, Saniya's favorite snack, and there was no light to microwave the child a Betty Crocker mug treat. So, Nagma decided to take her stepdaughter out for a breath of fresh air. It was pouring, and the little one excitedly put on her eye–popping, neon yellow rain suit which came with adorable black boots. Nagma's heart melted. She promised herself that she'd raise Mehmood's daughter like her own. They told the driver to stay in the house, for they were just going for a stroll in the park. Saniya jumped in every puddle she could find, and not once did Nagma stop her. Her attention towards her doting stepdaughter was disrupted by the whispering winds almost tingling the insides of her ear lobes. She often imagined that the strong winds carried with themselves creatures, and it was those things that made the whooshing sounds, for they did not want people to leave their houses. She never did like the wind; it was just the piercing raindrops that soothed her.

Nagma sat on the bench and let Saniya run around the swings. She told her to not go too far and that they'd leave in ten minutes. And so, with those instructions, Saniya jumped from one wet slide to the next. That rainy night, Nagma and Saniya were the only two in the park. The other people were inside their houses, with their windows shut tight and drapes hung loose. The other people also had caring husbands.

After some time, Nagma noticed that Saniya was on a seesaw, high in the air. It was too dark for her to make out her step daughter's expressions but she thought that she was stuck, and that she might be weeping. There was no one holding her up, no one on the other side of the seesaw – just air, and the air could not be heavier than chubby little Saniya. *The jhoola must be broken.*

Nagma walked towards the child and asked her if she should take her off the swing.

"Beta, yeh aisay nae letay. Ap tou uper hi hou gae ho. Yeh uper jata hai. Phir neechay jata hai. Aao main utaroun," Nagma insisted. But the child wanted to be stranded in the air. She shook her head.

"Mujhe pata hai, mama. *Wou jaan booch kar mujhe uper rakh raha hai, mama,"* the child uttered. Nagma stared at the swing in disbelief. She had read a fair amount of child psychology, and she knew that children tended to make characters in situations they did not quite comprehend. *Ab aik bachi kou main kya physics kay laws samjhaoun.*

And just then, in front of Nagma's eyes, the seesaw started to move up and down–up and down. The wind brushed through the strands of Saniya's curls as she guffawed in delight. Saniya's legs were spread in front of her, not making any movement, but the swing itself swung her up, and then brought her down. Before Nagma could register what was happening, the movement of the seesaw accelerated greatly. Up. Down. Up. Down. Up. Down.

"Ma–aa–ma–ama *j–jjj–ee!"* Horrified, Nagma grasped her daughter from behind and dropped her to the ground. Her silk *dupatta* was caught in the seesaw which was aggressively going up and down, and Najma ran towards the house without her belonging, with Saniya clutched against her chest.

Saniya wasn't bruised, but she began to sob profoundly, just as she was doing so before the incident had taken place. Nagma ordered food for her, and tucked her in bed soon after. Nagma stayed up all night herself.

The next morning, she went to open the door for the guard and the house help. She hadn't forgotten about last night's occurrence but at that point, she just wanted to rid the house of the dust and catch up on some sleep. Rubina, the maid, when stepping inside, handed a roughly wrapped cloth to Najma.

"Yeh kya hai?" she asked.

"Baji, gate say atka huwa tha apka laal dupatta. Maine jaldi say pakar liya takay ur na jaye. Raat ko hawa ki waja say...,"

Najma examined the *dupatta.* It was the one that she had left hanging on the seesaw in the nearby park. For a minute, she stood looking at it, not knowing what to do. Then, she told Rubina to wash it with the rest of the clothes.

The wind could not have delivered my cloth across the road, across three turns, to my house. It couldn't have.

Days passed and Nagma's mind relaxed. She forgot the happening like one forgets any other bad dream. On Sunday, Mehmood came back and greeted his wife and daughter. He was in a good mood and since such a mood was hardly expected, Nagma smiled and sat down with him.

The *azaan* could be heard inside the house and just as soon as it started, Mehmood got up and told his family that he's taking them for breakfast. It was noon, and they decided to walk towards the *naan channay* joint. This was the first time they were having something that didn't cost 10,000 Rs. Mehmood had always been reluctant to try desi dishes from street vendors, and Nagma thought that Gujrat's winds had done him good. It was also the very first time that Mehmood held his wife's hand whilst they walked alongside the road. Perhaps her absence had made him grow fond of her.

They ordered *nashta* and talked about Nagma. They talked about the storm, and about Saniya's education. And just then, the driver called Nagma. Thinking that it might be regarding Rubina wanting to s*ki*p work and go home early, she picked up. She would have never picked up anyone's phone during such a delightful morning.

"Baji? Sahab ghar aa gae hain. Pooch rahe hain kay ap kahan hai aur Saniya *bibi kahan hain. Guseh main hain, baji,"* Rubina said. Confused and angry, Nagma told the driver to put *'sahab'* on the phone.

"Nagma. *Yeh kya mazaak hai?* Where are you, and where is my daughter? I deliberately told you not to leave the house without Kamran driving you guys. Come home at once!"

Nagma placed the phone on the wooden table and looked in front of her. There sat Mehmood, grinning, with his eyes a pale and feverish yellow, not blinking. They widened by the second.

She quietly held Saniya's hand, hurriedly turned around, and led her towards the house. She felt like she was being followed, but she did not dare look back. During this time, she kept reciting the *kalma* as rapidly as she could. Or was it a surah, she did not know; she just kept taking God's name.

And now, she sits with Mehmood during their dinners, separated by a plate of barbecue prawns, longing for heartfelt communication, wondering if the jinn that the winds had brought to her that Sunday were indeed a gift.

Naveed got divorced after two years of marriage. He didn't blame her. Rameen was a good wife and a good mother, but she believed that her son was possessed by the *sheytaan.* Naveed believed the reports that clearly stated that it was autism. And so, whenever young Shayan repeated a word forty times without blinking, Rameen would start reciting the Quran, and Shayan would begin to wail loudly as a result.

"Apko nahin pata. Wou ghoor ghoor kar, gutne maror kar bol raha tha, Naveed."

"Kya bol raha tha?"

"Aurat sharbat day. Aurat sharbat day."

"*Tumhara damagh tou theek hai,* Rameen? Are you out of your senses? He can barely speak, and he repeats one word and you lash out on him for misbehaving? That's probably why he cries, poor thing."

"Naveed ap–"

"Bus karo, Rameen. *Bus ho gae hai meri.* If a child repeatedly asks for a drink, you give it. You don't bring religion into it!"

And that was it–Naveed's last straw. At first, it was just a separation. But then, when Shayan would return from his mother's with cuts on his face, Naveed filed for divorce and demanded the child's custody.

He felt upset for whatever had come between him and Rameen–whatever it was that had made her take it all out on their poor son. Sure, Shayan repeated things, he yelled, and he screamed; he stared at people and urinated when shouted at, but that did not mean that he had a jinn in him. A part of the child reminded Naveed of his childhood. He had always been the quiet child who had stammered his way through school. He had to be homeschooled in the USA later on.

So, it was a fine Wednesday–one of those mid–week Wednesdays when Naveed had everything sorted out–he had finally managed to tell his boss that he'd be working from home now, except if there were server emergencies, in which case he'd be at the office. He had taken Shayan out of the autistic center, dedicating his time to his son. He had brought his mother a plane ticket to come from Karachi to help him out.

Rameen had been Naveed's mother's choice–

Begum Iffat's. Begum Iffat was a meddling woman. She

wanted everything done according to her choice, be it the table's mats or her son's wife. Naveed had grown fond of a German girl back in the States, and Begum Iffat had slapped the girl when she had seen her sitting on Naveed's lap. She had then flown her son to Multan, where Rameen's family was stationed, and Naveed had gotten married.

Begum did not like her grandson. She believed that special children weren't children, and Naveed's white German ex–girlfriend had cursed Rameen's *goud.* She flew to Multan to help Naveed but made it clear that she'd not be looking after her grandson. And so, day after day, she made scrumptious treats and desi *khaanay* for Naveed and his son, but not once did she look at Shayan, or pat him affectionately, or make him the meetha pharatha she always made for her other grandchildren.

One day, when Begum was peeling potatoes for Nadeem's *manpasand* khattay *aloo*, Shayan came and stood by the kitchen counter. The house help was washing clothes on the other side of the kitchen's net door. The sun was shining to its fullest, and the Begum's *taez aanch wala choola* was making her sweat through her *lawn ka jora.* Begum spotted Shayan at once, nibbling the shredded carrots.

"Chalo andar jao, shabash," she said. Shayan continued to munch with his mouth open.

"Beta, andar jao. Forun. Chal." The little boy looked up and spat the carrots from his mouth onto the counter. *"Satyanaas hoye tera chawaleya!"* Begum grimaced.

Shayan stood there watching as Begum threw the carrots away and slapped him on his back.

"Chal. Andar ja. Chal!" she repeated. Shayan quietly made his way inside.

At night, Begum couldn't sleep. It wasn't the light, or the slow fan, or that one fly in the room that occasionally buzzed in her ears. It wasn't the bed or a bad dream; it was her hand. At first, she thought that the weight of the gold bangle that usually adorned her wrists was weighing down her old bones, but then, the pain pierced through her veins. She was up all night trying to press her right hand under her back. It was the most uncomfortable night of her life.

In the morning, when there was enough light to see clearly in the room, Begum saw that her hand was swollen like a *gubara,* the type the vendors in Murree fill with water to be shot at with guns. Her hand didn't hurt anymore, but it was full of discharge.

Naveed immediately took his mother to the doctor. Medicines were given. Bed rests were advised. At home, the house help said the oddest thing to *begum.*

"Baji. Yeh koyi bemari nae hai. Humare gaoun main na aik mard ka aisa hi haath soojha tha. Kehte they uski ragoun main nasli jinn dhorta hai."

The only person who was amused by dadi's huge hand was little Shayan. He even drew it on one of his copies and laughed every time he came across it.

The very next day, Begum woke up to find Shayan sitting

on top of her. Before she could react, he slapped her across the face. It wasn't like getting slapped by a child. It wasn't like getting slapped by Naveed's father–it was a thousand slaps at once.

"Budhi. Iffat. *Budhi. Chali ja. Buddhi,"* Shayan groaned, and his eyes turned white, like Begum's dry–cleaned guest room sheets. His voice wasn't his, but an old man's. Begum Iffat, who considered herself to be the strongest woman in the family, fainted after feeling both terror and pain.

At the end of the week, it was just Naveed and little Shayan sitting in the lounge, looking at different shapes of clouds.

Kehte hain, Naveed never found out the truth about his son. But, if he ever did scold him or hurt him, he suffered a heavy loss. On days when he was a good father, money appeared in his pocket, and the smell of fresh zarda filled the corners of the house.

Chapter 2

Muhabbat and Jinns

A collection of short tales following the territories of forbidden love, coupled with the *erotic* horror of humans adoring the creatures that fondly roam among us. Mixed with a hint of tragic poetry, each story knits back pieces of hearts torn apart and promises lost. We love so dearly; sometimes, the heart beats faster hearing someone's name, and other times, it slows down at the sound of it. That's what *muhabbat* is–it's unpredictable, like a rainy day. *Kabhi madham madham si,* like a soft touch on the cheeks; *kabhi taez si, jaise unki nazraein.*

❶ – Bhaari Naam

Zeerak. That's what her nani wanted to name her. There was no deeper meaning to it. Her nani had once had Zeerak, a boy, work for her and he made the finest *karhae wale kapre.* And so, when her daughter was expecting a girl, she wanted to name her Zeerak–firstly, because of the worker boy with magic in his hands, and secondly, because she loved zeera biscuits. During the ninth month, her nani sent out all the mithae and cupcakes with white–colored frosting, all of them crafted with the word Zeerak.

Sadly, before Zeerak was born, her nani died. And that sealed the deal: her name would always be Zeerak because it was her late nano's *aakhri khuwaish.* When Zeerak turned nineteen, as rebellious and as keen as she was to get a nose job, she decided to get her name changed instead.

Zeerak. Sounds like a terminal illness. Usay zeerak hou gaya hai.

And in the midst of autumn, when all the trees shed their leaves, Zeerak shed her name. To the world and to herself, she became Zania – modern like the icing on the cupcakes announcing her birth in 1995. It started with her changing her name on Facebook, then getting her certificates altered, and it ended on the wooden initials plastered outside her bedroom door.

Zania was a corpulent girl, and her skin wasn't her best friend. But, she had all the confidence in the world and it overshadowed her appearance. She had a good set of friends, and she could make the best *jhaag wali* chai. There was nothing extraordinary about Zania.

The instant Zania turned twenty– two, *rishtas* started

pouring in for her. Some would call, others would visit, and some would meet her. But all of them, in the end, would leave.

"Zania *beti bohut pyaari hai,"* the *rishte wali aurat* would *say. "Sab pasand karte hain usay,* Zubaida, *likun pata nae kyun koyi rishta nahin hou pata."*

The *rishte wali* aunty assured Zania's mother that there was, in fact, nothing wrong with her daughter. She had lost weight and her skin was clearer; they had a good house, and she did impress all of the aunties.

During that time, Zania started becoming inclined towards her cousin, Aamir. He had returned from China after having studied medicine and was staying at his taya's house. It was a short stay, but in that span of six months and *dhaki chupi mulakaat,* Zania and Aamir developed a strong li*ki*ng for each other. At night, Zania would help get the mattress for Aamir bhai due to a constraint of space, and in the morning, she'd make him poached eggs–a recipe that she had learned on YouTube.

Aamir's ami was a sweet woman. When she noticed that her son fancied his cousin, she talked to Aamir's abu. Thinking that the *rishtedaari* would be strengthened further, he happily agreed.

Both Zania and Aamir were over the moon. The *khushi* could be seen glued to their faces. Time was short and preparation was a lot, and during the hassle of buying the furniture, Zania fell ill. This wasn't the type of illness that brides usually go through though–she wasn't having second thoughts and she certainly didn't have food poisoning from eating Liberty market's street food. She was seeing things.

At night, she said that her cupboard would open and her clothes would walk. As absurd as it sounds, and as hard as it is to believe, it did happen, and the moment Zania decided to make a video, the *shalwar kameezain* which were walking in straight lines, collapsed on to the floor. Then, her ami started to sleep with her. During those nights, her thumbs hurt. She couldn't describe the pain to the doctor, but she tried:

"It's like, doctor *sahab,* there is someone in my room who places an inches tape in my hand at night, the kind that rolls back in once you are done stretching it. She asks me to hold on to it. She then goes on to stretch it right till she reaches the kitchen, and lets it go. It reels back in and snaps at my fingers with great pressure."

The doctor examined her nails, and each nail had a little cut on it. It was more of a bruise, and just to experiment, the doctor bought a rolled–up measurement tape and told the wife to stretch it and leave it upon his signal. The tape came rolling back at great speed and struck the doctor's pinky finger. Of course, it hurt. And doctor *sahab* got a little mark on his right pinky, just like Zania's.

During the next visit, he told Zania to let go of the tape before the creature did. Of course, in front of Zania's ami, he just spoke about the ointment that her daughter had to apply *din raat.*

Soon, the *purasrar* issues weren't confined to Zania's room. The salan in the kitchen started going bad, the lights started to go out, and no one in the house seemed happy. The *Qari sahab* who taught Zania's younger brother Zain advised the parents to call in a *Mufti sahab*. Hesitant at first, the family agreed.

"Nazar shazar lagi hou gi. Mufti sahab theek kar dain gay."

After examining the house and Zania, *Mufti sahab* told the family that as astonishing as it is, Zania's name is *bhaari*. It's not that girls can't be named that; it's just that it didn't go well with her personality, and perhaps changing it would help.

Zania believed otherwise. If there was anything that she adored more than Aamir, it was her four–year–old name. And so, she decided to keep it.

"It's just mumbo jumbo, ami. *Kya ap bhi na,"* Zania insisted.

That night, as Zania lay under the ceiling fan dreaming of herself as a bride, her slumber was disrupted by a loud, crea*ki*ng noise. Concluding that the fan was making the sound, she turned it off. Every night, the fan caused the same racket. One particular *raat*, she decided to stare at it. So, she sat on the bed, staring at the fan spin around like ami's sphere churros being deep–fried, swirling in yesterday's oil. Zania gra*dua*lly drifted to sleep. As usual, the disturbing sounds woke her up. She flung her eyes open and caught a bird's eye view of the fan. Sitting like a frog on one of the fan's arms, spinning in circles, was a woman staring at Zania. The spins were too fast at first, but eventually, on its own, the fan slowed down.

"Ami. *Wou ghoom raha tha phunka,*" she said to her mother. "*Khud hi ahista huwa. Uper aap bethein thein. Magar apki ankein sufaid thein aur apka moun khula huwa tha. Ap maindak ki turan bethi thein. Phunka ruk raha tha. Mujhe laga ruke ga tou apki humshakal ki back meri taraf hou gi. Per wou ruka aur us aurat ka moun meri taraf tha. Usne moun neechay kiya. Dekhti gae mujhe. Muskarate rahi.*"

It took some days for Zania to recover from the incident. She was surrounded by flowers, including floral designs adorning her *jahez* clothes. Aamir was taking good care of his *dulhan*–to–be as well, which acted as a catalyst in the recovery process.

One afternoon, outside the Askari Five Street, where Zania would usually roam around with fresh *roti* in her hand, she saw a girl limping and walking towards her. Without a second thought, Zania started to walk fast, towards that girl, so that she could catch her for scaring her like that – to vent out her frustration. But just as Zania walked faster, the girl turned around and started to run towards Zania. She wasn't limping anymore. And her feet...under her long, torn frock, were twisted. With those feet turned backward, she ran forward. She ran past Zania, who was frozen in shock, and the wind that followed the strange girl smelled like uncooked eggs.

That was the last straw for rebellious Z. She sat her family down and changed her name back to Zeerak. It felt as if fifteen kilos of weight had been lifted off her shoulders. That night, she slept peacefully and woke up next to a pack of half–eaten Zeera biscuits at Fajar time.

❷ – Modern Pyaar

16th May. It was the first day of Ramadan last year. Two things happened: Warda felt incredibly happy after losing her child, and Munazza felt appalled after being left alone with her older sister's son. These two women, Warda and Munazza, looked quite similar and yet they had drastically different personalities. Both of them used Maybelline's sand shade to cover their *ubtan* colored skin, were short and surprisingly, had green eyes – though Munazza's glowed under the moonlight and Warda's were dull but attractive.

Warda Jamshed married the love of her life. Her parents were conservative, and so, it took years for her aba *hazoor* to agree to a man who wasn't his choice. Warda's ami made it clear on the day of her daughter's valima that no matter what happened in her marital life in the future, Warda couldn't come crying to them; Azaan was her choice after all.

And so, the first time Azaan hit Warda, Warda let it go. The second time, she cried silent tears. The third time, she swallowed the *garam aanso* down. The fourth time, she locked the door, knelt, and wailed loudly. Eventually, she lost count. Days went by and the marks remained–like *mehndi* stains from the salon in the society no aunty goes to because their henna has chemicals.

Azaan would come home, completely in his senses, and bang Warda's head against the rusty brown drawers that her abu had given her. The drawers were originally there to stock her makeup and garments, but now, they stored bruises and dried blood blotches. At night, Warda would brush his hair back till he'd fall asleep in her lap. Both of them would wake up for Fajar, pray, and then go back to bed. Warda would carefully fold the *jaynemaaz* so that Azaan wouldn't slip in the morning, for if she did disappoint him, he would pull apart her fingers till her throat would run out of energy to moan for forgiveness. *Khair*, the couples who pray together, stay together.

Four years of an abusive marriage, *loug kya kahein gay*, and three miscarriages later, Warda got pregnant. For many weeks, she was oblivious that a *nunni munni jaan* was growing inside of her. The nausea that occurred, she mistook for the aftermath of her sedation pills, and her cravings for a chocolate cake she fulfilled by putting melted Dairy Milk on an old fruit cake stored in the fridge.

Old sad songs continuously circled her mind, and her body felt itchy. It was only when *saath wale ghar ki* Rubina said that she felt in her gut that Warda had the *noor* of a baby boy on her face that Warda went for a pregnancy test. She got those forty–rupee strips from chacha Bashir's pharmacy, and for two consecutive mornings, she peed on them. Both times, it was positive.

Azaan, upon hearing the news, brought home Warda's favorite meal from Hardee's. They were going to celebrate over mushroom burgers and an episode of Narcos. The truth was that Warda despised mushrooms. She said that it was her favorite meal only because Azaan would have pulled back her braid for being *nashukri*. And at that moment, because of the pregnancy sickness, Warda puked. She wiped the previous day's *channay* off her mouth, put on lipstick, and headed back to take another bite of the mushroom–infused treat. Azaan was happy, and so was she.

The beating did not stop. Azaan said that it would. But then, he decided that Warda was indeed a *chawal aurat*, a *naish* being, and a *manhoos biwi*. Two slaps at noon and one in the night keep such women in their *aukat*.

Warda wasn't a halfwit like this narration may seem to suggest. She was an *akalmand insaan*, and she knew that even with the baby, the *maar pitae* would not end. Possibly, Azaan would hit the child as well. Warda knew it well. And so, she prayed day and night for God to take the child to heaven before it could open its eyes. On some nights, with swollen lips, she told her eight–month–old stories of Jannah's gates and rivers of honey so dense that no one could drown in them; you could eat the honey while floating in it.

What followed in the busy streets of Karachi is a story

that *dadis* tell their *bahus* so that their son's wives remember to be thankful, the likes of stories that men like chacha *jee*s mention over *karrak* chai. The listeners nod, try to believe the tales, and go on with their lives.

The day of the expected delivery was near, and Azaan was in a rotten mood. It was either because of the hot weather and the wind carrying broken promises back to the beach, or the fact that Warda could no longer move and serve her husband *jamasheri*. The pains had started, and each time Warda groaned, she made her voice turn into those Ding–Dong bubble–gum jingles. Eventually, she persuaded Azaan to get up and take her to the hospital.

"Apka bacha abu say milna cha raha hai, yaar," Warda said as she felt fluid dripping down her trembling thighs. For the first time since her pregnancy, she wanted to keep the baby inside her, protected and safe.

"Thora jaldi chala lain," she begged her husband while clutching her stomach.

"Kya kaha?" he utttered through his teeth, the grinding almost audible over the sound of the car's engine.

"Thora jaldi... Please," she begged.

Azaan smirked and started to decelerate the car below the speed of twenty. It was almost as if they were moving away from the hospital. *"Main aziyat main houn* Azaan," she said while gasping for air.

Azaan kept going in circles, and when he was tired, he decided to get the tires of the car checked.

"Azaan, please. *Mat karein*," Warda rolled over in pain.

"Bukwaas band karo apni."

Azaan stopped the car at the petrol pump and stepped out. As the door closed behind him, the gush of wind that made its way into the vehicle brought some hope with it. Tears flooded down Warda's flushed cheeks. Banging her head against the wall, getting dismantled under a speeding truck, burning herself with a melting wax candle, and starving herself–this pain between her legs was all of it at once. The worst part was that she was fighting it, trying to gather it inside.

She was fiddling with the radio button when a knock shifted her focus. A young boy, who looked like a window cleaner, stood outside. Warda signaled him to leave at once. The boy knocked again, and again. The miserable woman looked at Azaan, who was busy sniffing a cigarette with an old man. The boy started to knock rapidly, and Warda lowered the window.

"Please. *Paisay nahin hai. Chalay jayein*," she said to the boy.

"Paisay nahin chahiyen."

Warda started to sob hysterically. The pain had become unbearable.

"Royain mat. Ap bacha mujhe day dain. Beti hai."

Warda stared at the boy with a horrified expression, her eyes wide open. Everything around her had stopped. The radio had stopped; Azaan's movements had stopped; the cars driving past had stopped; the child pushing itself outside of her had stopped, and the pain had stopped. The boy–the window cleaner–and Warda were the only ones with blinking, moving eyes. Her surroundings looked like a scene out of her childhood. "*Aao* statue statue *khailain apa*," the boy smiled. Time had stopped.

"Ap kuch na kahein. Bus ijazat dain. Main apki beti dour lay jaoun ga. Jahan shehad kay darya houn gay. Wohi jinka ap isay btati theen."

There was an unexplained *noor* on the boy's face. It seemed as if he was made from sunlight, and sunlight alone.

Warda was shivering and she felt at a loss for words, but the tears that now left her eyes brought her comfort. The window cleaner put his hand through the door and touched Warda's stomach. It was a moment of bliss; a minute of Warda running through the corridors of her house with her aba chasing after her. *"Pakar liya! Pakar liya!"*

Warda allowed her heavy eyelids to droop, a drawn sigh of relief escaping her. When she opened them, the *shadeed garmi* had returned, the sunlight boy was nowhere in sight, and Azaan was making his way to the car.

"Haan bhai. Tou mar tou nahin gae?" he said in an amused manner.

Warda felt no pain. All she felt was *sakoon*. They drove to the hospital, and Warda delivered a stillborn baby.

"I'm sorry for your loss, Mr. and Mrs. Azaan. The girl is no more."

Warda looked at her daughter. The radiant sleeping beauty rested in peace, her warm pink cheeks just like a glimmering sun on a winter morning.

—

Munazza Mir, being the skittish woman that she was, painted the nursery a shade of yellow. She knew that Mubeen and Sijdah hated yellow, but she blamed them for not finding out the gender of the baby. *I can't put blue if it's a girl. Bus nahin.*

Girls may dream of being mothers, but Munazza always dreamed of being a khala. She was just fourteen when her older sibling Sijdah got married to Mubeen bhai, their second cousin. She knew how babies came in the world and every day, she'd ask Mubeen bhai if one was along the way.

"*Beta*, McDonald's *ki* delivery *nahin hai kay main* call *karoun aur aa jaye.*"

One day, however, much like a McDonald's McCrispy delivery from Y Block, came home a baby boy. Munazza had only found out about it during the seventh month because the family of now three had moved from Dubai back to Pakistan during that time, and she had been in little contact with them. With the sudden yellow nursery came all sorts of *jhoolay* and blankets. Munazza was jubilant.

And just like that, Munazza's list of boy names played a vital role in choosing young Sharan's name–little Sharu Paru.

From *jhoolay maiyan* to khala's nap stories, Munazza was the perfect aunt, and it wasn't long before she became

Sharan's second mother. Soon, Sharan began to talk about tall buildings and the 'seeds' in khichri that he didn't consider food; young Sharu was growing up.

It happened to be one of those mid–December days when Munazza left for her AIESEC cultural exchange program to the Maldives. She promised Sharan a pet turtle, blue nail paint, slime, and a tablet that his ami would not allow him to keep otherwise.

When Munazza returned, she went straight to her sister's house. Sitting on his Peppa Pig bed sheet was Sharan, who paid no heed to khala's sudden arrival, or the packets of sweets she was carrying in her hands.

The room smelled like daal, and Sijdah informed her sister about Sharu's lousy *tabiyat*.

"The doctor *says* it's the *mausam. Hou jaye ga theek*."

But, Sharan refused to acknowledge his khala's existence. He wasn't interested in her, or the toys, and he certainly did not want to pause his tv–serial to get up and hug Munazza.

"Sharu. *Meri jaadu ki jhapi*?" Munazza urged. In two months, Sharan had become a different boy. His ami shook it off, but Munazza was not at ease. It was a week later that Munazza started to recognize the reasons behind her uneasiness.

It was *dophair*, and the entire *khandaan* had gathered at Sajida's place. She was expecting a second child, and Mubeen had just gotten a promotion which required him to shift back to Sharjah. Munazza sat next to Sharan, asking him if he liked the koftay she had made.

"Meatballs aur Doraemon, Sharan *kay* favorite!" Sharan answered in silence. Munazza followed Sharan's gaze and realized that he was staring at two lizards which had squirmed their way into the living room.

"*Ap fikar na karo* Sharan. *Main abhi inhe bhagati houn*," she said.

"Mat bhagana," he said. "Guests *hain meray*." Sharan's tone was ghoulish and grim.

Thinking that the boy was petrified of lizards as he had always been, Munazza ruthlessly sprayed the creatures with cockroach spray. Sharan stood there, staring at his aunty with lifeless eyes.

"*Haye* Sharu. *Aik tou ajeeb* brown *si bari chipkali thi. Mar dia isay.*"

Days passed and Sharan stayed the same. He hardly talked and hardly ate anything except boiled chicken botis. He no longer found K&N's dinosaur shaped nuggets appealing. He needed copious amounts of meat, otherwise he would not eat. The Snickers bars in his cabinet went untouched.

Come first of Ramadan, Sijdah and Mubeen left to get their passports attested, leaving Munazza in charge of Sharan.

"Popcorns *khaein gay*. Iron Man *dekhain gay*. Snapchat filters *say* photos *lain gay*!" Munazza squealed.

Maasi Munawar was sitting in the garden peeling old *kinoos* when Munazza entered the house. If she hadn't been on her period, she would have scolded the *maasi* for missing a fast. *These maasis, uff, they never fast–kamchor kaheen ki,* she thought.

Upon entering the house, Munazza felt dizzy. She had only slurped down a Shezan apple juice last night, and she blamed her hunger for not feeling up to the mark. Sharan sat on the viscose rug, blankly gaw*ki*ng at the wallpaper.

"*Meray* Sharu *nay kuch khaya hai*?" she asked dotingly.

Sharan didn't break his leer. Munazza sat down next to the skinny, pale boy. There, on the bronze–colored wallpaper in front of them, were two lizards. At first, Munazza thought of calling Munawar *Maasi* to kill them. But then, she noticed that the lizards were the same ones that she had slaughtered before: brown and *ajeeb si*. There was no doubt about it.

"*Ab na marna inhe*, Munazza. *Bura maan gae tou teray peechay ayein gay*," Sharan said as he shot her an unfeeling look.

Munazza stared at the boy and his unbrushed, parted hair, both in shock and disbelief. Sharan had never talked to her in such a manner. To him, she had always been Muzi khala. She took a moment or two to collect herself.

"*Beta, kin gande bachoun kay saath khelte hou aap?*" she asked and gulped. Her question was followed by an uneasy silence.

"Sharan. *Main dantoun gi ab. Itni buri baat hai–*"

Sharan started to breathe heavily, almost as if he was trying to lift heavy weights. His pupils started to dilate, and his gaze shifted from the wall to Munazza. His khala noticed the colors flush from his face. He tightened his fists and let his lower lip loose; yellow–colored, foul–smelling drool started to drip down the side of his chin. The little boy almost looked like an angry elderly man.

"Tu btaye gi mujhe, aurat? Tu btaye gi? Tu btaye gi! Tu btaye gi? Tu btaye gi!"

Sharan's voice sounded like a thousand men talking at once. Amidst his groans, his arms twisted sideways in an uncanny fashion, and he started lic*ki*ng his elbow. Shortly afterward, he straightened his body, picked up the lizards, and went upstairs.

Munazza stood there, swallowing her fear, examining the blood that furiously oozed out of her body and fell between her feet on the marble floor. At that point, it wasn't too far–fetched to believe that whatever possessed Sharan had caused her irregular periods and massive bleeding.

When Sijdah returned, Munazza left the house without any *salam* or *dua*. She just informed her sister about borrowing her *ferozi shalwar*, and that was it. A week later, the family flew back to Dubai with their son. Things remained as they were. Munazza got better, but she started to despise that time of the month. When it came, in a washroom, proofed with newspaper clippings and tape, it brought along two lizards to visit her. They stayed till she bled, and then they left.

On her twentieth birthday, her *saheli* said a rather nasty thing to her.

"*Haye* Maani. *Kya hou gya hai tumhe? Tum tou chipkali*

lagti ho–ajeeb brown *si.*"

❸ – Aam Aurat

She has a name that sounds like one of Abida Parveen's old songs. Perhaps her ami had her on a Sunday afternoon in the *aam ka baagh*. My Sami *jee* smells like mangoes when he comes home, so I assume that's the odor her body has–*kaate huwe aam, chilke kay begair.*

He speaks fondly of her–the way she's so shy that she can't look at him. And yet, she has him. Her eyes are purple, the shade of my valima dress. Nano Parveen used to *say* that *gulabi* rang isn't one for brides; it's the color of the old bowl in which we put our kheer and share it.

I share him. When he's with me, we have H market *kay* gol gappay; and when the *khatta paani* drips down his chin, he doesn't let me wipe it. But last Monday, I saw that the mole on his chin was covered with shimmery glitter reminiscent of the *sitaray* our clothes shed on Eid. He said that he had kissed her feet, her *khussas*; must have been the ceramic beads covered with silver powder. *I need to get rid of those khussas.*

Sami doesn't have a second wife. If he did, all the odd nights would have been mine–him and me on our clean Chen One bedsheets that I got on sale, draped in the comforter that leaves a scent that Sami adores. But now, he looks forward to the even nights and urges me to miss my

Maghrib prayer, so that on that *charpae* that I've now given to *Maasi* Kalsoom–the one that Sami's ami died on–so that on that very *munji*, he can lay down with me when I smell of aam. *Mousam ka pehla aam*.

Since I was little, she's been with me–when my *khussa* size was three, and the only *khussas* that fit were from the back of an old store at Liberty market. She had a weakness for those.

Papa *jani's* friend, *Qari–Sahab* Haider–I don't know where his grave is– used to read God's words out loud, and I would no longer yearn for *khussas*, and *aam*, and dead people's belongings. But he's gone, and he thought that she was gone. And one day, when I could still touch my husband's chin, I told him about her; and he wanted to see her.

"It's psychological," he said. "It's just your subconscious."

"*Jee*, Dr. Sami," I had said.

Then, I missed a prayer. I missed two. I missed five. I missed eight. Missed Maghrib prayers and eight *khussas* later, she came.

And now, my Sami is my Sami only when I smell like Sharaqpur's aam bag, the place where we met; the place where I swung the highest *jhoola* with papa *jee*, only to have my hair grabbed mid–air; the same place where I felt my body lift into the air and drop into a basket of mangoes. That noon, the three of us went back home – papa, me, and the woman that my husband loves.

Chapter 3

Darwaza khoul dou baby, and other stories

Quite often in life, we come across unexplainable things. They may be as little as who spilled the box of Olpers milk in the kitchen when you've only ever stocked up on Prema milk boxes, or as monumental as hearing your dead mamoo's cries from your nano's room. They may be as eerie as dreaming about the same cashier you will happen to see at Sapphire the next day, despite never having met the man before. Except that in your dream, he held a blood–stained lawn print instead of the *gulaabi* one he would be holding the next day. These unexplainable things may be as formidable as knowing that when you lay awake at night unable to move your limbs, it's not sleep paralysis but a lingering entity inside your room in the hours before Fajar.

These things happen, sometimes quite often and other times, not so much. But they can't be explained, and so we live with them, trying to make logical excuses, blaming our minds or the *kharab* channay in the gol gappas we had last night for making us hallucinate. But tonight, we shall record such riddling experiences of the mind, body, and soul before we can shrug them off as bad dreams and nothing else– so that we may retain some semblance of sanity.

The first tale is shorter and older than the others but it seems like yesterday's narration. Hania Shafiq was a frisky soul. She combed her hair a hundred times, never with a brush, and believed that this way, her frizzy hair would turn silky smooth– like a cluster of ironed threads. Her father was conservative and believed that she should not leave the house without an *abaya*. Half her life, she had struggled to unfold her trousers before her father came home because she wasn't allowed to show her ankles. When she got married, it was a transition from a narrow street to a grassier playground, the type her brother used to play football in. She had all the freedom in the world. Her husband just wanted her to listen to him talk about his day every night and yearned for Hania *kay haath k banay huwe* gobi parathas.

In exchange for that, Hania was allowed to wear what she liked and act how she pleased. One night, Hania was coming home from dinner with her friend. She wore skinny jeans, the kind that painted themselves on her legs, and a yellow floral shirt that could attract bee stings. Casually, flexing her legs, she got out of the car. She flipped her hair over her shoulder stylishly, and upon turning her head to the right, noticed a *molvi* sahib standing quite still, staring at the ground.

Thinking that it was because of her clothing that he wasn't looking at her, she sighed and said *salam* nervously, for the *molvi sahab* reminded her of her father. The bearded man, who seemed to be in his late fifties, did not reply. Hania repeated her greeting twice and waited for several moments for him to answer her. He didn't, and so she went inside.

She changed into her green *shalwar kameez*, a night suit that she had dedicated to nights spent in comfort, and listened to her husband speak about his day. Hania was troubled; she felt that the *molvi sahab* had not answered her because of what she had or had not wrapped around her. She slept perturbed, wondering whether her father would have acted in the same manner as the *molvi*. In the middle of the night, Hania woke up with chapped lips. With her eyes partially shut, she fiddled around to find her spectacles. She then walked towards the small dispenser in her room and waited for the water to fill the glass slowly.

Her husband was fast asleep, and the room smelled like the aftermath of too many gobi parathas. Hania gulped down the water and went back to bed. She was awoken shortly by a feather–ish tingling on her feet. It felt as if someone was playing with her toes. Her husband was still fast asleep next to her. She got up and, quite suddenly, jumped back. There stood, at the corner of the bed, a dark figure slowly moving its hand around her toenails.

Hania put on her glasses and threw her legs under her husband's body for protection. As the figure moved closer, she saw a somewhat familiar face– it was the *molvi sahab* who had not responded to her *salam* some hours ago. He looked much older than before, and it took Hania a minute or two to regain her senses.

"Sorry jee. Jab apne pehle salam kiya tha tou main ankhe khol kar sou raha tha. Walaikum as salam, Hania!" After whispering this, he passed through their bedroom wall, like an evaporating cloud of dust.

The second tale is a recent one. I like to call it, *"Darwaza khoul dou, baby."* That is what Hussain used to *say* when he'd come back home from a night with friends. Hussain and Fatima had been lovebirds at LUMS, a university where they were both average students, yet happened to ace the communication skills class, which, as it turns out, did not surprise their parents. They got married when they were both twenty-three, a young age, the age of freshly baked bread– when the relationship is hot and fragile.

Hussain worked at Maple Leaf, and Fatima liked poetry, so she quit her job to write about the relief her luxury *shaadi* sheets and feminism gave to her. They wanted a baby, a little bundle of joy, to watch British cartoons and talk in an accent whilst living in Lahore. Hussain loved dressing up babies.

If he hadn't been an accountant, he would have opened up a Minnie Minors' franchise. Hussain, like any other lad his age, had a considerable number of friends. He was the life of the party; the candle to a birthday cake, the *jugatbaaz* from Faisalabad, and a pro at Rang.

Fatima's *saas* said that once she'd have a growing jalebi in her belly, Hussain would stop going out in the late hours of the night. Fatima didn't mind. She was fine with her husband's inclination towards a good game of cards, a friend to roast and chai at *dhabas*. She believed it kept his mind young. The only problem Fatima had, however, was having to open the door for her husband at three in the morning. You see, her *saas* and *susar* would be fast asleep, dreaming of their younger days; the maids went back home at nine; the driver, Jamshed, only stayed back on Sundays ever since late–night phone calls to his beloved turned into *shaadi*, and the *chokidaar* never picked up his phone.

Hussain couldn't ring the bell; his amma held her restorative sleep dear so that her Ponds age rejuvenation cream would have its full impact. His only option was his obedient wife, lying in bed eating the McDonald's he had bribed her with. So, each time he went to his friend's house, upon returning, he'd call up Fatima and *say*, "*Darwaza khoul dou, baby.*" It wasn't as cheesy as it sounds now. It was after midnight, and the emphasis was on the *darwaza* and not baby.

And so, every other day, Fatima would take the keys and

tip–toe outside. When, on some nights, she lay sleeping, she got frustrated at being woken up to open the door. On other nights, she'd make Hussain agree to shopping sprees, for there was nothing nastier than a night of interrupted sleep.

It was a February night. The lawn fever had started, and Fatima was ordering herself Zarah Shahjahan's Dhoop Kinaray prints online. She was like that; picky about her prints, conscious about her brands, and she always did choose till after midnight to order.

After making substantial use of Hussain's online finances, Fatima drifted off into a content slumber. She was awoken by the sound of Phil Collins, her phone's ringtone. Collins soothed her, just like long bubble baths and meetha anda with cinnamon for *nashta*. She read the word, 'Husband' on her phone and emitted a long, stressed, sigh.

"*Jee*?" she said.

"*Darwaza khol dou, baby.*"

She got up, took the keys, and opened the door. She then came back and went to sleep. After what seemed like an hour, her phone rang again–Tarzan's theme song. She picked it up.

"*Jee koun*?"

"Hussain. *Darwaza khol dou, baby.*"

Fatima got up and rubbed her cheek. *Hain? Yeh phir kahein nikal gae they?*

Shrugging her shoulders, she got up, took the keys, and opened the door. She then came back, told him not to turn on the lights, and fell asleep. Soon after, the phone rang again. Phil Collins did not seem soothing anymore.

"Koun yaar?"

"Hussain *houn, jaan. Darwaza khol dou."*

Fatima sat up, fully alert. She turned on the lamp and checked her call log. Before this call, the only call she had gotten was from Warid. *Yaar yeh kya hou raha hai?*

She got up, took the keys, and opened the door. This time, however, she stood by the gate to see Hussain drive the car inside. Hussain looked at Fatima and smiled. Satisfied by her husband's return, Fatima dragged her body inside and jumped on the quilt. The clock struck four, and the phone rang. Fatima's eyes flung open, and she stared at her vibrating device. It was Hussain. Hesitantly, she picked it up.

"Haa–haan jee?"

"Darwaza khol dou, baby."

Fatima looked at the clock, really stared at it, for a good minute or two. She memorized the time and went outside. No matter how awake she wanted to be, she was in a sluggish state, and it all felt like a bad, repetitive dream. Fatima opened the door and her eyes followed Hussain driving the car inside. He had the same expression on his face; in fact, the only thing different from her previous memory of opening the door was Hussain's smile; it was wider this time. Fatima waited for him to lock the gate and the car and walk inside with her. Hussain hugged her, and they went inside. Fatima felt emotional, so, they made love under the warmth of her *saas*'s quilt and the humming of the electric fan. Fatima hugged Hussain from behind and they slept like two lovebirds.

In the comfort of the hot room and Fatima's happy state of sleep, her phone rang. Knowing that Hussain was right next to her, with her eyes shut, she picked it up.

"*Salam. Jee?*"

"*Darwaza khol dou, baby.*"

Fatima felt a shiver run down her spine. She jumped in fright when she looked to her side and witnessed an empty bed. She was wearing her nightie; a cloth she had confined only to making love. She quickly wrapped her shawl around her and ran outside. She opened the door and saw Hussain drive in. His smile was wider, wider than it had ever been. Instead of letting him in, she ran back inside and locked the main door.

She then locked her bedroom door and hid inside the quilt. She lost track of time and how profusely she was sweating, and soon found herself drifting off. Fatima woke up at nine in the morning and found Hussain sleeping next to her. She woke him up and spoke about the insidious night before.

"*Kesi baatein kar rahi ho?* Hussain stared at her in confusion. "*Kal tu* abu *ne darwaaza khoula tha* because your phone was powered off. Plus, I didn't feel like waking you up or calling abu inside because you were in your nightie, *yaar*!"

Fatima sat back and looked at herself. Her clothes were

scattered on the floor on the left side of the bed, not hung on the stand; she was wearing something she never actually wore to sleep, and her phone–well, it was powered on with no less than 85% battery.

The third story is like *ghee* on a *roti;* it's unwanted by some but required by a lot. Some people like their *roti* without *ghee*; dry– to be dipped in their cooked desi gravies; some believe a little *ghee* hurt nobody, whilst others bathe the batter in *ghee*. And so, just like *roti* and *ghee*, people's perception of this story varies. Muhammad Khan, a pious man, a religious scholar, and a loveable football player, was once asked a question by his roommate:

"Khan. You offer all your prayers. You fast, you give *zakat*, and you do *zikar*. You ask us to wake up for *tahajjud*. You're a good man. But in these past fifteen months, not once have I seen you wake up for *tahajjud*. Why is that?"

Khan looked at his friend and raised his unibrow. "If I tell you, you won't believe me," he said. The friend persuaded Khan to speak.

"I want you to tell me," He replied. "I'm very curious. I wake you up for *tahajjud*, and you refuse to open your eyes. Why is that so?"

Khan paused for a moment and then began narrating.

"This isn't a story. I believe stories can be fabricated. It's the truth, and truthfulness is just truthfulness–an occurrence, but not a story. Long before I became a man of religion–long before I was guided towards the one true path, I used to wake up at *tahajjud* to help my father capture pigeons. He would do *parhai* for days, sometimes months, and meat was not allowed in the house during that time.

After the *wazaif* would be complete, we'd go up at *tahajjud* time and capture a flock of pigeons. I never questioned him; I never questioned the time, or why it was always pigeons and never crows or sparrows. They'd be flying just above our heads, and we'd grasp them tightly. Then, baba would take them inside. Our ami and sisters had strict orders not to come out of the room until the early hours of the morning.

But I'd see large men in our house. They were so large, brother. They'd have bulging white eyes with no pupils and no eyebrows. They could stretch their arms and legs in an ungodly manner. Abu would talk to them, and then he'd put *taweez* under the pigeon's feathers and set it free. Those creatures would fly till they reached their destination and then would drop dead just miles from it. I learnt that it was *kaala ilm* and even after learning what it was, I practiced it and so now, I can't wake up for tahajud, for when I do, I see pigeons without heads, and they come at me; they poke their bent beaks in my eyes till I bleed. It's a punishment."

Muhammad looked at his friend and burst into tears. His friend, sitting across the room, extended his hand, and stretched it till it reached Muhammad. Just like the large men with no pupils.

Chapter 4

Horror Stories for Children

"Traumatize your child! Ladies and gentlemen, traumatize your child once and for all!"

The lady with the corkscrew curls and the Khaadi bag hanging on her shoulder ran across the streets of Lahore, selling stories that the world had not read before. It was past midnight and the shops were closing. It was odd because Lahore never slept, at least not till three in the morning. I knew so because that's when I ordered the Hot and Spicy's 'after–twelve' paratha roll deal. I looked at the woman in confusion. She appeared to be in her early twenties, and each time she ran fast, her loosely hung *shalwar* was pulled up.

She seemed like a lunatic, running around, trying to sell stories for children at that hour. "It's a wicked night," the man behind the counter said, "I've already put my children to bed." I took my paratha roll from him and headed home. *What a weird lady,* I thought to myself. I walked down the street, gobbling up the cheese behari wrap, careful not to let the sauce drip on my new shirt.

The wind was rather chilly, creating rattling sounds and blowing through my unwashed hair. When I reached home, I locked the door behind me. I went straight to my bedroom to tell my wife about the strange lady selling ghost stories for children. My wife smiled and said that her stories weren't that bad.

"Of course, I haven't read them. They're for children," I replied, "but who writes ghost stories for children and offers parents to buy stories that'll send their children to therapy?"

My wife smiled again and pointed towards Sana, who was staring at the fan.

"What's wrong with her?" I inquired, pinching my ten–year–old daughter. She just wouldn't stop staring at the ceiling.

"Baba," she whispered, "mama read me new stories. I can't sleep, baba." My daughter was shivering. I looked at my wife in horror. She sat in peace and after a moment, she slid her hand under the bed linen and took out a familiar book. It was the book the crazy lady had been selling on the streets.

"Let's read these to Sana together," she said. Her nose twitched, and blood started pouring down from her ears. It poured down on her blue *kurta*, right down to her shoes.

"Haha!" Sana laughed, "Blood, baba. Let's play in blood!"

These stories are jinn tales based on real creatures and set in even realer surroundings. They're to be read aloud to your children at bedtime. They've purposely been written in a childish manner for your child's little brain to comprehend, and for your adorable child to be disturbed for years ahead.

❶ – Best Friends

Once upon a time, in the crowded streets of Model Town, there lived Mr. and Mrs. Khan with their beautiful daughter Pinky, and their dog Rani. Rani was much older than Pinky. Pinky's real name was Pareesa, but her cheeks were so rosy red all the time that the neighborhood aunty Shaista started calling her Pinky, and soon everyone forgot Pinky's actual name.

Mr. and Mrs. Khan had spent a great amount of time childless, and so, for the longest time, Rani had been their only companion. Until Pinky turned seven, all was well. Rani loved the child, and the child loved Rani. After Pinky's seventh birthday, which was held at Gymkhana, a membership Mr. Khan proudly flaunted, his daughter changed. She no longer liked meetha anda; her cheeks turned a shade of yellow; she started to dislike sitting on Mr. Khan's stomach for *jhoole maiyan*, and she started to growl in an unsettling way every time Rani came near her.

"Our Rani's so sad," Mr. Khan said, "she refuses to eat,

being abandoned by Pinky like that."

Mrs. Khan frowned. She was a woman of much sense. "It's a dog, Pinky's papa. A dog!" she said, combing her daughter's raven hair.

Mr. Khan noticed that Rani had started to spend an awful lot of time barking outside Pinky's bedroom door. *Woof woof,* she went, day, noon and night.

"The dog's broken," Mrs. Khan said, one Sunday afternoon.

"What nonsense," her husband replied. "How can a dog be broken?"

Their chatter over chai was disrupted by angry snarls coming from upstairs. The parents ran to attend to their daughter. They sprung open the door, only to find Pinky giggling by herself.

"Oh, sweet child," Mrs. Khan said. "Whatever was that noise?"

At first, Pinky didn't answer. She felt amused seeing her parent's startled faces.

After a moment of silence, she got off her bed and pointed towards the roc*ki*ng chair.

"My best friend just told a joke!" she chuckled.

Both Mr. and Mrs. Khan looked at the empty roc*ki*ng chair in puzzlement.

"Perhaps our daughter has an imaginary friend," Mr. Khan whispered in his wife's ear. "Let's play along."

After that day, whenever Pinky pointed at walls, Mr. and

Mrs. Khan looked, whenever she laughed, they laughed and, most importantly, whenever she asked for more kheer for her best friend, they gave it.

Months passed, and Pinky started losing interest in school. Mrs. Hafeez, her teacher, came to visit the Khans one Monday morning. She was a tall woman and she wore giant spectacles that covered half of her face.

"Mrs. Khan," she said, sipping her Kashmiri tea, "your house seems rather odd."

Thinking that Mrs. Hafeez lived in a smaller house without a dog and a servant, she assumed that Mrs. Hafeez was jealous.

"I have been blessed by God to sense evil," Mrs. Hafeez continued, "and I sense something sinister in your house."

Mrs. Khan chuckled in delight. "Pinky is a smart child. She will improve her grades." *Or else, I'll change her school.*

Mrs. Hafeez placed her cup on the polished, brown table. "You don't understand," she replied. "I came here to talk about Pinky but I am more concerned about the wellness of this house."

Mrs. Khan escorted Mrs. Hafeez out with a bag of roasted almonds that she gave each of her guests.

"Have a good day!" she said before shutting the door.

A week later, Pinky was down with a fever. She couldn't eat, she couldn't sleep, and she looked very weak. Mr. Khan had her daughter checked by the very best doctors, but none of them could point out the sickness. Mrs. Khan pressed her cheeks against Pinky's and fed her the family's traditional herb soup. The soup didn't work either. On top of it all, Rani just wouldn't stop barking.

"My dear child," Mrs. Khan wept, "what has made you so feeble?"

Tears trickled down Pinky's plump cheeks. "It's my best friend, ama. She's free."

Troubled by what her daughter had just said, Mrs. Khan spent the night awake. She went to the dining room hall and took out a supara. She didn't own a Quran Majeed, and she felt awfully guilty about it. But, she had *suparas*, and so she took out the first from the pile. She covered her head with a silk *dupatta* and sat under the light of the lamp.

I will pray to God. God will make my child well.

It had been a long while since Mrs. Khan had recited God's words. It took her some time to stop stammering, but eventually, she did. The moment she regained fluency, she felt a gush of wind blow through the room. The windows were closed and she stared at thin air in astonishment. There was no one around. She continued reciting, and in about a few moments time, Mrs. Khan felt that her feet were off the ground. Quite literally, they were off the ground!

Startled, she jumped off the couch that seemed to be levitating in the air. She was swearing profusely, and even though she could smell Johnson's baby powder, someone or something else could smell her fear. Clutching her pashmina shawl, she turned around and gasped in fright. Under her couch, holding the sofa above its head, was a creature that looked like a little girl. It had no neck, and it was all over the place.

The face appeared to be a child's, but when looked closely, it seemed like that of a crow's. Its almond–shaped eye sockets were hollow and black, and even though it had no eyes, Mrs. Khan knew that it was staring right at her. She flung her shawl into the air and ran outside as fast as her corpulent legs could carry her.

The next morning, she told Mr. Khan what she had seen.

"You must have had too many pakoras before going to bed," he answered.

But Mrs. Khan knew what she had witnessed. After her husband left, she went upstairs to discuss the matter with Pinky.

"Mama," Pinky said, "don't be scared of her. She's my best friend. She won't hurt you." But Mrs. Khan wasn't so sure. She had Pinky's teacher called to her house in the evening.

"Mrs. Hafeez," Mrs. Khan said, excusing herself. "I am sorry for the inhospitable–"

"No worries," Mrs. Hafeez spoke up. Her glasses slid down her face. "It isn't your fault."

So, Mrs. Khan told Pinky's teacher everything that had happened since Pinky's seventh birthday. She told her about Rani's sudden sadness, about Pinky's growls, about her daughter's illness, and most importantly, about Pinky's best friend.

"Hmm," Mrs. Hafeez said after listening to Mrs. Khan's story, "it looks like a jinn has been invited into your house."

Mrs. Khan choked on the samosa that she was eating. She coughed till she spat the *aloo* out.

"Oh my! A jinn? Whatever for? I would never invite a jinn for tea let alone have it in my house!"

"Jinns," replied Mrs. Hafeez, "don't work this way. Especially satanic ones that cause chaos. Pinky must have invited it unintentionally and now it's feeding off of your emotions."

Mrs. Khan hurriedly went upstairs and fetched Pinky. Pinky was still a little feverish, but tucked behind her mother's *kameez*, she followed her downstairs.

"Don't call her it," Pinky said. "She's my best friend. She's been here for years now."

Upon inquiry, Pinky told the ladies that when she was seven years old, she had gone with Zulfiqar uncle to the park. She had found a pretty Barbie bangle lying under one of the swings, and had brought it home. Once she wore it, she'd often see her best friend. She didn't name her anything, she just called the creature her best friend.

The creature would brush Pinky's hair, slither her tongue down Pinky's throat, and play hide-and-seek with her. After some time, she asked Pinky if she could fetch gosht from Mrs. Khan's freezer. "But you like kheer," Pinky had said. The creature bit Pinky on the shoulder, so Pinky got her the meat. The demon had then asked Pinky to invite her to have the meat, and Pinky had done so.

"Mrs. Khan," Mrs. Hafeez spoke up, "it looks like the jinn was attached to the foreign object that Pinky brought home, and bit by bit, it associated itself with Pinky–and your house. The reason it showed itself to you yesterday was because you tried to remember God, and the devil can't stand God's name."

Before Mrs. Hafeez could continue, Pinky picked up a samosa and chucked it in Mrs. Hafeez's eye. The crisp fell to the ground, covered in a sticky, iris like substance. Mrs. Khan screamed and slammed her body against the wall in an attempt to step away from her daughter. Pinky, now possessed by the entity, ground her teeth together and clung onto the wall. She crawled across the wallpaper with oily hands and jumped on her mother. She bit the skin off of Mrs. Khan's face, bit by bit, till Mrs. Khan stopped screaming. Then, she squealed in joy and crawled back upstairs to the room. No one knows what happened to Mr. Khan and Pinky afterwards. Some *say* that Mr. Khan ran away with Rani, whilst others *say* that the best friend killed them all.

❷ – Mithae

Anum was a good girl. She got straight A's, and her long legs ensured that she was a star in her aerobics class. Her ami thought that she was too old for aerobics, but Anum did it anyway. She was much taller than normal nineteen–year olds, and her ironed straight hair–parted in the middle–fell till her shoulders. She originally belonged to a *gaoun* outside Lahore, but she hardly had any memories of that. The only things that she could recall about the small village were how summer hardly paid it a visit, and the odor of the horrendously pungent oil that a *Maasi* from the village had applied in her hair.

Anum had eyes the size of majestic bees, the kind that are only found near sunflowers grown from burpee seeds. Her ami often said that Anum got her eyes from her great grandmother, Chachy Zubaida, the woman who wore no saree unless it was the color of gold and made her eyes look like blossoming sunflowers when she flung it under the village trees. Anum knew what Meer meant in his *ghazals*, she knew how integration worked, and she definitely knew how beautiful she was.

Anum had it *all- khoobsurati,* a loving family, two great *sahelian* Palwisha and Mano, and a great career ahead of her. But Anum also had a secret. A secret that terrified her to the very core of her existence. It was the winter of 2002, and young Anum was a chirpy, hyper child. The days were shorter, and the nights longer. Those were the days young Anum happily sat in her father's mithae shop, giggling with a mouthful of rasgullahs. Mr. Aamir had always been fond of two things in life, his love for mithae and his *gur se meethi* Anum.

His house was right next to his shop, and the location

was the very best in town. People from different cities used to come to try Mr. Aamir's *sheeray wale* gulabjamun and jalebis that never lost their crisp; his sohun halwa that was better than Multan's finest, and his *garam* chum chums which sizzled when placed on the tongue. Word got out, and soon, the elite from Dubai were visiting Mr. Aamir's mithae shop. When the Sultan had a son, he sent a man to collect the best kaju barfi and milk laddu from Mr. Aamir's shop. That's how blessed the shop was.

"The thing about jalebis," Anum used to say, "is that they have to be rushed from the shop to my house. Only at this particular distance do they stay this yummy. Other women reheat them. And reheated jalebis are never the actual jalebis, you know?"

For some time, the children gathered around to hear the stories of spiraling golden jalebis. But then, Anum stopped telling them. She became rather quiet. She stopped being the excited Anum that she was because of her secret. That secret made little Anum *sheera*–less. It was another morning, and Anum was jumping excitedly, telling her abu about an art contest. Chacha Bukhari was assembling the team for that day's orders, and Anum had taken a day off from school. She was sitting by the window, looking at things happen. Multiple families sat in the room. They were casually dipping their sawaiyan in fresh milk–except one family.

The woman who sat in the corner was staring at Anum. The man who was sitting next to the woman, who appeared to be her husband because they looked nothing alike, was staring at Anum as well. The child that the woman held in her arms, was looking at Anum too. Their food was getting cold, and yet they sat still, staring at Anum. Of course, little Anum felt weird. The woman looked younger than any of the women seated in the shop. She was beautiful too, and her head was partially covered with a *dupatta*. Her eyes were green or maybe, it was the light above her head that made her eyes look that color. But they certainly weren't black like Mr. Aamir's, or brown like Anum's. And that is when little Anum noticed that the woman wasn't blinking, neither was her husband, and nor was the child. Anum had been told that it was rude to stare, but Anum started staring back. Blink, she thought, blink. The woman didn't blink, the man didn't blink, and the child, who appeared to be a baby boy, certainly didn't blink. They sat, peaceful as ever, staring at Anum without blinking.

Anum looked around to see if others had noticed them too, but everyone was too busy to listen to her. So, like the child she was, curious as a cat, she went up to the woman. The woman, with her eyes wide open, welcomed Anum into her arms. Quite unexpectedly, the woman's jaw dropped into her lap, and her eyes went upwards. It was an otherworldly sight for little Anum. She hadn't seen any horror movies growing up, but she had just read her first Goosebumps book, and nowhere did it talk about a woman whose jaw fell right down.

Startled, Anum screamed. She screamed as loud as her lungs let her. Mr. Aamir jumped from behind the counter to aid his screaming daughter, who was lying near the only empty chairs in the mithae shop. For the next few days, Anum wasn't herself. She had a high temperature, and for the first time in her life, unwashed, sticky hair wasn't her biggest worry.

"Papa," she asked, "why doesn't the doctor uncle believe me?" Mr. Aamir held his daughter's hand.

"I believe you. *Ab jaldi jaldi theek hou jao. Mithae nae khaani?"*

But Anum knew, deep inside of her, that what she had seen could not be forgotten. Anum did get well again. She forgot the face of the woman and her family over the years, but after that day, she never visited her abu's mithae shop. She was scared that she'd see the woman, the child, and the man again, and that once more, others around her would not.

On her nineteenth birthday, many years after the incident, her father brought home a rather charming family. Anum had known Mr. and Mrs. Bilal's son since childhood. Yasir was twenty–five years old, and he had just completed his masters. He had a great job, was a nice man who offered his prayers five times a day and vowed to keep Anum very happy. Anum agreed to the rishta, and so, it was settled; Anum and Yasir would get engaged on Anum's twentieth birthday.

Mr. Aamir was delighted. As the days of the ceremony

came close, Anum had a sinking feeling in her heart. She liked Yasir, and she had full faith in her father's decisions, like all good girls should. But, she had a constant fear of going to sleep at night. The fear was rather weird. For instance, whenever she'd close her eyes to shampoo her hair she'd think that something might enter her from her nostrils. She thought that when she'd try on a shirt and raise her arm to put the shirt on, someone or something might clutch her arm and pull her upwards. She slept with her *maasi* in the room. She thought that when she'd go to turn off the lights, there'd be someone sitting on her bed.

She no longer wanted her cat to give her kittens; she thought that one of the kittens would limp and then turn into an old man. She thought that when she'd sit on the toilet seat, something would go splash in the water under her. Her reasons were rather uncanny, but she had them; so, she felt like she was never alone. Her father showered her with gifts, *choorian* which went well with her dress, gold that made her sparkle in the moonlight, maids to accompany her after marriage. Mr. Aamir even arranged for main market's Waffles by Alamgir to be present at Anum's engagement to hand out fresh, special cones topped with roasted nuts and chocolate that hardens because it was his *beti's* favorite.

One day before the engagement, Mr. Aamir asked Anum to accompany him to choose which mithae she wanted in her engagement boxes. The special red laddu from which Arabian *sheera* oozed out, the gulab jamun that floated in a pool of vanilla custard, or the magical ras milae which burst into rabri milk. Anum wanted her father to choose, but Mr. Aamir did not take no for an answer, taking Anum along. During the one–minute walk to the shop, Anum felt her legs getting heavy, as if her body did not want her to take another step towards the shop.

But of course, she did. She let out a sigh of relief upon reaching the shop. It was crowded, and she wasn't alone. It had been years since she had entered the shop the last time. The entire structure had changed. The place smelled sweet dark but sweet. In the middle of the shop stood pillars with mirrors on them. As Anum passed them one by one, she felt quite odd. She stepped backwards and took a look in the mirrors. In the first mirror she passed, she could see that she was wearing a traditional *lehnga*, much heavier than her engagement dress–and that had been the heaviest in the market. In reality She wore skinny jeans from Outfitters that she had ordered online but in the mirror, it was a traditional *lehnga*.

Wrapped in laces and pearls, stones with rainbow colors, laced with real petals, it was the kind her eyes had not seen before. In the second mirror she passed, she saw that she now wore a *chholi* to go with the *lehnga*. It fit her. It fit her better than any of the shirts she owned. It felt as if it was made just for her. The third mirror that she passed showed a *dupatta* on her head. Her face no longer looked dull; it had lit up, and her eyelashes were as long as ever, shimmering with glitter that had fallen down to her cheeks. Her lips were red. She had never worn such a bold color before. The crimson red was redder than the blood a paper cut had given her, redder than the glowy signal outside the shop, redder than – tomatoes. Chillies. Her favorite *kameez*, roses, apples, meat, strawberries ripe from the baag – redder than anything she'd ever seen. She licked the red with the tip of her tongue to see if it would come off. It all seemed imaginary, anyway. Real, but imaginary.

The red did not come off; instead, her tongue had a taste of heaven, like all her *salgirahs* had come at once. The red on her lips tasted like a hundred of her abu's mithai all together in her mouth, making love to her tongue. She stepped ahead, and there were no mirrors. It was indeed the strangest thing that she had experienced. She chose her mithae and went home. At night, she tried her engagement dress. It had been crafted to perfection, but now, she wanted that *lehnga*. The *chholi* she had seen herself wear in the mirrors of her father's mithae shop.

She started to try on the shade of all the lipsticks that she owned. Mind you, she owned many. She mixed colors to form a red, but it was never that red. And her lips tasted like... lipstick. Anum didn't feel happy.

The next day, when *Maasi* woke up, Anum wasn't in her room. The *Maasi* woke the other *Maasis* up. Anum was not in the house. She was not at the shop. She wasn't at the parlor, and she wasn't with Mr. Aamir. The house was searched, the footage was watched. They saw Anum sleeping peacefully in her bed. And then, the footage stopped. Each camera stopped. Mr. Aamir was alarmed.

Children, Anum was never found. Mr. Aamir looked for her. The police looked for her. The entire population of Lahore looked for her. No one knew what happened but us. You see, when Anum was little, the woman that she had seen had been a jinn. Her husband had been a jinn, of course, and that little boy who didn't stop staring–you guessed it right–had been a jinn. They couldn't blink because, children, jinns don't blink. The woman had shown herself to Anum because she had chosen Anum for her son. The baby jinns, they grow faster than humans. The family had been regular customers of Mr. Aamir's mithae shop. Jinns, they love mithae. No sweet shop in Lahore isn't visited by *hawaei* creatures at night. The jinni, before Anum's engagement, had taken her away for her son. What Anum had seen in the mirrors had been a glimpse of herself as the jinn's bride. It's a secret, but we'll tell you. The mithae at Anum's wedding to the son of a two hundred–year–old jinn had been from Mr. Aamir's mithae shop.

❸ – The Kabristaan

Children, one day you'll go through something worse than a paranormal experience. More terrifying than the jinns living in your washroom. More horrifying than multiple *sheyateen* possessing your younger sibling. More frightening than a churail hanging from your living room ceiling fan. Scarier than the dwarfs on your chest that wake you up from your summer nap during *dophair*. More startling than the footsteps you hear after Maghrib. More alarming than the baby boy that rides on your back when you go down for *sujood*. More terrifying than the second ami who rocks you to sleep and lives under your bed.

That thing, my children, is called heartbreak. Humans are creatures of clay. Gullible, foolish and weak. They listen to the heart, and not the sounds of nature and thus, their heart destroys them. *Dil ki baatein. Dil main basay loug. Kahein ka nahin chorte.*

There used to be a *qari sahab* who lived in Defence, Lahore. He was married, and he had two children, a beautiful daughter and a handsome son, Amara Meharunisa and Ibrahim Sherbahadur respectively. The *qari sahab* was quite rich, and the other men who taught the Quran often spoke of his story amongst themselves.

"Ali Sherbahadur teaches the sons of jinnat," they'd say. "They bring him pots of gold and *aloo* and *gobi*, and chicken with aromas outside of this world."

And children, that is partially true. *Qari sahab* had pots of *sona* and pots of *chaandi,* and also food that made Amara and Ibrahim lick their lips for days, for it was quite extraordinary. But, *qari sahab* wasn't a happy man. He used to sweat on winter days, when the cold would be too much to handle. He used to shiver during May nights, when there would be load–shedding in Lahore. His daughter Amara would often ask him what the matter was, but he'd change the topic and request tea from her. Amara would bring the tea and *qari sahab*'s *manpasand* bakar khanian, and even after having them, the *qari sahab* would still not feel at ease. It was as if nothing could make him relax.

In the autumn of 1985, when *qari sahab* had married Parveen bibi, a girl from his village, he was at his happiest. He oiled his beard, woke up and went to the masjid when no one would be awake, and he gave away most of her earnings to schools. Parveen bibi was a petite girl, seven years younger than *qari sahab*, but approximately the same height. Often, years later, they joked about how, with heels on, *qari jee* looked like a midget next to his wife. Their jokes were precious. When Parveen bibi was pregnant with Amara, *qari sahab* would take her out to the city for spins, and she'd giggle when the wind would blow away her shawl.

Riding on her husband's motorbike, clutching him from behind, the scent of his strong *itar* spiraling around her nostrils, she enjoyed her favorite time of the week. They'd often go on rounds and sip a can of Mirinda from the same straw. *Qari sahab* wouldn't mind if the straw was stained with shiny, pink lipstick, for they were very much in love. Then came Ibrahim, their second child, and though Parveen wasn't petite anymore, though she grew fond of Limopani, which was available in their village, and though there were no more motorbike rides, *qari sahab* still adored his wife. He wished to gift her jewels one day.

"I'll gift you *sona* and *chaandi,"* he'd say. "But, nothing would be as beautiful as you my *jaan."* Parveen would blush. *"Ap bhi na!"*

One day, when *qari sahab* returned home from teaching the village children, Parveen asked if she could learn the Quran as well. The *qari* agreed, and every day after Maghrib, he'd teach her. To his astonishment, not only was his wife a quick learner, but she had the most magnificent, melodious voice while reciting the Quran.

The leaves stop rustling to listen to her tilawat. Time stops, and everything comes to a halt. Ibrahim stops weeping, and the hair on my skin *stands up. It's a wondrous feeling. So, this is what jannat will be like; The Quran and my Parveen.*

Between the qari's house and the school he taught at, was a graveyard–a *kabristaan*. The *kabristaan* was very old. The *banyan* trees situated there hung too low. *One day,* the *qari* thought, *they'll collapse.* It wasn't well kept, and the graves were hidden under heaps of dirt. One night, the *qari* was hurrying home. He had gotten late because one of his students had become a Hafiz–e–Quran and had treated him and the other students to samosas. As the *qari* hurried through the *kabristaan*, he flung the packet of samosas and chutney for his family.

The night was young, as it was almost Maghrib time. Quite oddly, by the time the *qari* reached the middle of the *kabristaan*, he felt as though the *kabristaan* had just started. He took long, wide steps and again, he stood in the middle of it. The *kabristaan* wasn't ending! No matter how much he walked, he just couldn't cross it. Soon, the *adhan* for Maghrib time began. The *qari sahab* saw that multiple men, with large, broad chests, and shadows larger than their bodies appeared from behind the wall. They had white beards that shone, and they walked with their eyes wide open, fixed on the ground.

"Ghabrao mat". They said. "Do not be afraid. We bring no harm."

The *qari* gulped and hid behind one of the *banyan* trees.

"Do not be afraid, Ali," they repeated. "We are the creatures made of what lies between the day and night. We come in forms of corpses that lie under this ground. We are Muslims. We believe in God and His Prophet, but we are not humans, and we are not jinns. We are what you cannot see and what you cannot know. We will give you worldly goods if your wife will teach our children the book of God in her melodious voice. In time, she will return on her own to you."

The voices were coarse and heavy, and *qari sahab* was shivering. The 'people' soon vanished and the *qari* hurried back home. He did not like what he had heard. but truth be told, he wondered what worldly goods he might get. He slapped the back of his hand for thinking such a horrid thought. *Parveen. Meri jaan.*

When the *qari* reached home, he was drenched in mud

and salty rain water. He opened the door to find Amara and Ibrahim playing with clay on the carpet. They had no clue where their ami had gone, only that someone left daal and chawal on the front door. The *qari* tasted the rice and the gravy, and felt himself tremble–both with pleasure and fear. The food was extraordinary, and its scent had filled the house; but he wanted to know where Parveen was. He put milk on the stove and waited for his wife to return. After what seemed like ages, but was really only minutes, he told his children to stay put and went to search for Parveen. He looked in the garden, and in their small house, in the neighbor's house, in the shops, in the school, in the hospital, on the roads, and even in the *kabristaan*. But, Parveen was nowhere to be found.

After that day, *qari sahab*'s health deteriorated. He felt like he was only alive because one day, Parveen would be back. Years passed and no one came. The city men bought the *kabristaan* and intended to make a school there, but *qari Sahab* set fire to the blueprints and scared the men in the darker hours of the night.

The kabristaan. My Parveen will return from the soil in the kabristaan.

The *qari* had stopped teaching the Quran, and as troubled as he felt by it, he'd stopped opening God's book. His small house changed into a bigger one. His garden grew the largest lemons – the only lemons the village had. The qari's family always had food. Plenty for themselves, and plenty for whoever visited.

When Amara turned eighteen, the *qari* decided to marry her off to a tailor. The tailor was a religious man, and he lived in the nearby village. He sold fine silk and presented the *qari* with all shades of silk when he came to ask for his daughter's hand. That night, the *qari* dreamt of something rather daunting. He dreamt that he summoned dark spirits and offered them his daughter whilst she was dolled up in pink silk. The shadows took her and brought back Parveen. The nights to follow had the same coldness to them, and in that coldness, the *qari* dreamt of the horrid creatures.

On the day of Amara's marriage, she wrapped herself in the tailor's finest pink silk. On seeing how familiar she looked, the *qari* listened to his *nufs*, the *sheytaan* inside of him. He quickly locked the doors and slit his wrist. He smeared the blood on the ground started to chant in what was otherwise complete silence. He did not know what he was saying, but he knew that it was not what he had been taught. He then took his daughter to the *kabristaan*.

"Abu? Why have you brought me here, abu? Abu, please. What is this? Abu, are you missing ami? Abu, please. It's night time. Abu, I smell of *ubtan* and *mehndi*. Abu, I need to sleep. Abu, take me home."

The *qari sahab* dragged his daughter and threw her on top of the dirt. He could feel on the tip of his tongue that the air he was breathing in was that of twenty years ago. It started to pour. Amara began to sob hysterically.

"My abu has gone mad," she said. "My abu has gone mad."

Soon, Amara stopped. She sat quietly near her father. As the *Qari* chanted, Amara danced. She had not done the devil's deed before, but she got up and swung her body in the air. She danced with her feet, with her arms, and with her chest. She was not Amara. She danced for the moon and the night. Her eyes changed to a shade of silver, and they sparkled from far away. Her lips went inwards, and her hands curved backwards.

"Nachwa. Nachwa. Raat kay andhere main nachwa, budhe!"

When the sun came up, the *qari* dropped to his knees, sucking the dew drops from the isolated rose growing from the grave in the middle of the *kabristaan*. His daughter's body lay near him, lifeless. She had a burnt triangle on her back–something that had been embedded into her flesh, it was the mark of *sheytaan*. Maggots fed on it.

The *qari* rubbed his eyes and looked around him. He did not spot Parveen. But as odd as it may sound, he felt her near. Barefoot, he ran back home. The house seemed strange. It felt dull, there was no food on the table and the cracks on the walls were evident as ever.

A week later, the *qari* died of a horrid pus infection. He got boils all over his body that no doctor in the city could treat. The moment they cut a boil off, another grew. No one could lower the *qari* into his grave because he smelled of dead rats.

❹ – The Womb

Kiran always preferred Faisalabad over Lahore. She liked that the traffic was much better, and that *shaadis* could go on till after ten. Her friends lived in Faisalabad, and the best gola ice–cream that she had ever eaten was also in Faisalabad. The ones in Lahore topped the gola with Rooh–Afza only. Kiran could never make any friends in Lahore. She'd joke and people would get offended. *Haye Allah. Mazaak hi tou tha.*

When she turned twenty–two, she got married and moved to Lahore. It was very unpleasant for her. On top of the environment, her *saas* was a very loud woman who only had one question on her mind. *Khush khabri kab aye gi?*

Her mother–in–law had four sons and three daughters, and she expected Kiran to have an even bigger family. The bigger the *khandaan*, the merrier. Fortunately for Kiran, her husband, Sohail, understood. He told her to relax and said that with time, God would bless them both. Soon all of Sohail's brothers got married. *Dulhan* after *dulhan*, Kiran miserably decorated other people's days, scared that they would have a child before her. One time, she even Googled ghastly things:

How to make your dewrani lose her child if pregnant please tell

How to make your jethani never have a child please tell Google

Sohail's youngest brother had twin girls. The middle one

had a daughter. The older one had a baby girl too. But, Kiran had no child. Her *saas* sent her to the best doctors, but all of them said that both husband and wife were well, and that there were no complications. Yes, children, the doctor tells when the baby is on its way. The bird your abu tells you about is just a bird.

Kiran's mother pressed her fingers against Kiran's forehead and told her to close her eyes. Frustrated and with warm tears rolling down her cheeks, Kiran sobbed to her mother. She told her about how every time she got her period, she wanted to kill herself. The next day, Kiran unwillingly had to take her *bhabhi's* twins to the park. She watched children play amongst themselves, and push each other and lick ice–lollies. She badly wanted one of her own. At the park, under the clear blue polluted sky of Lahore, she felt better.

She decided to take the children to the park every other day. She started to notice that each time, the children and the parents would be different, but one particular old woman would always be sitting near the water tank. Her skin looked like an old date, wrinkled and brown. On the ninth day, the old woman came up to Kiran. Thinking that she wanted money, Kiran extended a ten rupee note towards her. The old woman took it and smiled.

"*Meray liye dua keejye ga.* I want a child."

The old woman gave a toothless smile and went away. That month, Kiran did not get her period. She ran to the doctor, with much excitement and hope.

"Congratulations," the doctor said, "you're six months pregnant."

Six months? But how could that be? Kiran went from one doctor to the other and all of them told her the exact same thing, she'd have a baby in three months. Puzzled, she told her husband to take her abroad to get a checkup.

It's been six days. I can't be six months pregnant! How absurd. I don't even have a tummy!

Before Kiran's visa could arrive, she started to feel sick. If she got a cut, no blood came out. Her hair grew longer and her skin glowed. All of the fillings in her mouth fell out, but she did not visit the dentist. She liked how her tongue could enter the holes between her decayed teeth. The scent of meat made her sick, so all she had was mixed vegetables; *aloo matar gajar.* Sohail felt scared about his wife's condition, but he knew that with pregnancy, every woman's case is different.

There is a scientific explanation. She was pregnant but she did not know. The child is making her sick. It's the beauty of life. It'll be over before she knows it. Come on, Kiran. We've wanted this for so long.

Kiran would lay on the bed and count her days. She would imagine the little toes and the little fingers and a beautiful face. *My baby will be beautiful.* Kiran was sure that it'd be a boy. No one else gave a boy to the family. I'll give a baby boy. A *waris*. Kiran's maid also told her that it'd be a boy because of the shape of Kiran's stomach. And for the first time in years, Kiran's *saas* was overjoyed. She was calling everyone she knew, telling them about Kiran's boy.

What showed up as the eighth month on the reports, was the third month of pregnancy for Kiran. They got the upper portion of their Wapda Town house polished and furnished. Kiran now felt the baby move and kick. It was a terrible feeling because each time she felt the child move, she had a panic attack. *Jaise gale main boti phuns gae ho.* Sohail had taken a leave from CureMd, the software house he worked at. He wiped Kiran's vomits and helped her dress every day. He could not help but notice how odd his wife's body had gotten. He had, of course, seen his bhabhis' pregnancies, and none of them looked so dreadfully proportioned. The most unspeakable part was the fact that Kiran never peed. Days went by and she didn't pee, and whenever Sohail told her to force herself to use the bathroom, he himself would have the most nightmarish time in the washroom- pee that burnt, solid excretion that made his body tremble. He knew that something was awfully wrong.

One night, Sohail woke up to see a little boy sitting on the edge of his bed. He held a parrot in his hand, and as Sohail moved upward from his sleeping position to see the boy, he saw that the boy was half - human half - horse. He had hooves. His complexion was white, and he smiled at Sohail. Sohail, after witnessing this harrowing sight, jumped from the bed. He recited *dua*s, but the boy did not move. He tried to wake his wife up, but Kiran had always been a heavy sleeper. He picked up the boy from his hairy, horse like legs and dragged him outside of the room. He then closed the door. He was shivering. He quietly got into bed without washing his hands.

Weeks passed, and Kiran stopped talking. She occasionally ate, painted her nails, and believed that everything was well. Sohail and his mother got a doctor to attend to her in the house. An afternoon before this, I must mention, Kiran's eyelashes came off, and because of no protection around her eyes, her eyes inflated to the size of little gumballs.

"Bohut ajeeb case hai. The patient isn't responding. I think we should take her to the hospital immediately, Mr. Sohail."

And so, they did. They rushed Kiran to the hospital. Kiran requested the doctors to let her use the washroom before any treatment. They insisted that a nurse could help, for Kiran had gotten so weak and fragile. She looked like a wilted flower, half devoured by hoverflies. Kiran went to the washroom and closed the door behind her. She held onto the sink and turned on the faucet. She then began to push. The first minute went by smoothly. The second minute felt like her body was being swallowed whole and in the third, she started to feel her body lose the weight. The fourth minute, she stared at the ground and there, on the bathroom floor, covered in blood, lay a beautiful, giant, baby lizard.

Kiran picked it up and kissed it. "My beautiful winter child. *Mera jaan ki tukra."*

❺ – Helper Aunty

Kae yaadoun kay chehre hain
Qissay puraane hain
Teri sou dastaanain hain
Teray kitne afsaane hain
Magar aik wou kahani hai…

Zubaida turned off the music and looked towards the street. It was empty. It wasn't that late, at least not for Zubaida Arif. It was only eight, but Islamabad slept early. The weather forecast had predicted rain, and the air was humid as ever. With sweaty hands, Zubaida shoved the phone into her back pocket and crossed the street. Her feet hurriedly made their way towards the footpath. She wasn't a fast walker. In fact, she was quite slow in every aspect of life, which is why the marketing company she worked at had suggested she continue on as an intern.

But, Zubaida was sure that she'd get the job. She needed the job. A year ago, she had all the money, and she would get her beloved cheesecake from Burning Brownie each day. But now, she could hardly afford to have it once a week. And, the cheesecake had turned into a chocolate cake slice because her three–year–old hated cream cheese. After her divorce, Zubaida was keen on making ends meet for little Yahya.

Careful not to step on the cracks, believing it to be a bad omen, superstitious Zubaida stopped midway. Bloc*ki*ng her path, sat a beggar with a child in her arms.

"Baji jee. Beti bohut beymaar hai. Paisay day dou. Allah kay naam per paisay day dou."

Zubaida flung her *chaddar* sideways, and continued to walk. Beggars irked her. If she could work with a son and no support, they could too. *Why should they get money by just asking? I work day and night, and I don't get a loan–hadh hoti hai wesay.*

She turned around. She couldn't make out the face in the dark, but the figure was that of a woman's. The area around her was stinky, and her dark hands were grubby. The beggar was sobbing, with a child wrapped around her waist. The child seemed quite alright, perhaps even peacefully drowned in a slumber. In her subliminal mind, Zubaida was Thinking about why each lamppost spanning the street was lit, and only the street light above the beggar wasn't. *Maybe she chose to sit here so that no one would recognize her. Taubah, beggars.*

"Salam?" she said. The woman looked up and wiped the mixture of snot and tears dripping off her chin.

"Baaji... beti bemar hai. Madad kardo," the woman pled. Zubaida frowned and bent down. She didn't have any money and even if she would have had some, she wouldn't have given the woman any. *Hatti katti lagti hai. Gharoun main jaa kar kaam kare,* she thought.

So, as surprising as it may sound, Zubaida knelt for a good ol' five minutes, and lectured the beggar about how she should work, and how no one sane would buy the 'my child is sick' drama. She told her about how she worked day and night so that her son would have his favorite chocolate cake, and that the beggar could do that too.

Zubaida hadn't lectured anyone before. Not even the man who had cheated on her, or the parents who had told her that she was a *bouj*. But, it was as if it all came out–all at once. Every bit of it. The beggar had her eyes fixed on Zubaida's shadow, and the only responses she gave were sniffs and sobs. Having made her point, Zubaida left. She felt happy; she felt like she'd made a difference. She felt like she deserved a slice of Burning Brownie's cheesecake now.

The next night, Zubaida got off the bus, walked the same amount of steps to the sidewalk, avoiding the cracks, and again, stopped midway. She saw that the beggar she talked to was still there. This time, however, the street light above her was working, and she could see the beggar and the child in her arms clear as day. That night, the street light shone brighter than the moonlight.

The beggar was crying. It was a different type of crying. The day before, she had let out hopeless sobs; now, she was weeping hysterically. The woman could barely open her swollen eyes.

"Mera bacha mar gya. Kal kisi nay madad nae ki. Bachay kay kafan kay paisay day day koi," she said amidst sobs.

Zubaida was devastated, for she had made a terrible mistake. She had not walked past the beggar the other night. She had stood next to her and the dying child and had accused her of putting on a show. She had humiliated her and on top of that, not given her any money. And now, the child in her arms was dead.

Zubaida knelt hesitantly. *"Baji,"* the beggar pleaded, looking at Zubaida. *"Bache ko dafnane kay paisay day dou."*

Zubaida didn't know if it was the sadness of losing her child, or if the beggar truly did not recognize her. Trembling, she emptied her bag and gave the beggar whatever she had. She didn't remember clearly if it was a thousand or five thousand, but she gave it–every bit of it. Even the coins. Even her shaami kebab sandwich.

She went home, with tears rolling down her pallid cheeks. Her face was almost withered, and her makeup smudged all over. Upon reaching her house, she got into bed and hugged her child, Yahya.

A week passed, then a few months. The weather became colder and the days became shorter, and very soon, it became too cold to walk at night. There was hardly any gas in the morning, and so Zubaida and Yahya would have the previous night's Knorr noodles before Zubaida left for work. Her house help, who barely came anyway, left for her *gaoun* and little Yaha was left all alone. Zubaida tried taking him to the office, but he'd always throw a tantrum when his mother would pay more attention to the computer screen than his face. Moreover, little Yahya enjoyed going around spilling mugs of hot coffee.

Zubaida went home praying for some sort of miracle.

She couldn't work knowing that little Yahya was all alone in the house, and she certainly couldn't work with him around. It was Jumma, perhaps *Qabooliyat ki ghari,* and the struggling mother's prayers were heard. The bell rang, and Zubaida rushed to open the door with Yahya glued to her leg relentlessly. To her astonishment, in front of her stood the lady beggar who she had helped out of guilt a few months ago. This was the first time she had seen the beggar with tearless eyes and a relatively less swollen face. The woman was just as old as Zubaida, if not more. Her greasy hair was combed back and held together by a torn, faded sky–blue ribbon. She did not smell better, but she definitely looked better.

"Us din apne meri bohut madad ki thi," she said. *"Maine apne bache ko dafan kar diya. Aap apna shnakhti card bhi day ayi thein."*

Zubaida was speechless. The beggar handed her a few notes and her cards. One was a free meal voucher from KFC that she had been looking for, and the other was her CNIC. Zubaida looked at the hundred rupee notes in confusion.

"Yeh paisay bach gae they baji," the beggar said. Before that day, Zubaida had been particular by letting no one inside her house but her son and herself, and this one time, the plumber. But that day, Zubaida invited the beggar inside, and she even let her sit on her sofa. The beggar told Zubaida that her name was Kalsoom and that her husband had left her for a younger woman who worked in Karachi. Her son

had been suffering from seizures, and she didn't have any money to take him to the doctor, and just within two weeks, her son had died. She told her that people did leave ten–rupee notes and five–rupee coins, and she was ever grateful for that. She said that she had realized that time *tou likha hota hai sab kay jane ka,* and that she knew that her son was in a better place. She had made peace with it.

"Maine apko bohut dhoondha. Main apki bohut shukar guzaar houn." Zubaida understood that the beggar had not recognized her from the night she had left her son to die, and she thanked God. She brought Kalsoom Rooh–Afza and thought about how to repay her. Before Kalsoom could excuse herself and go out, Zubaida offered her to stay and help around the house – to take care of Yahya. Kalsoom was overjoyed. She did not expect any money. She cried tears of joy, and started work from the very next day.

Zubaida almost forgot that she had done this out of guilt. She was incredibly relieved. Kalsoom couldn't fry nuggets or make noodles, but she knew how to make daal, and so Yahya and Zubaida ate daal. She washed their clothes and cleaned their rooms. She let Yahya play *ghora ghora* on her back, and the best part was that Zubaida did not have to pay her.

One night, Zubaida woke up at three in the morning. Yahya had drifted off to sleep on top of her. She tucked him in bed and got up to drink water. With partially shut eyes, she went to the kitchen. She saw that Kalsoom's mattress in the living room was empty. The doors were locked from the inside, so she couldn't have crept outside. Curious, she went to the backside of the kitchen to check. She saw that Kalsoom was praying near the onion rack. Seeing this, she went back to bed.

The next morning, she asked Kalsoom why she had been praying at three in the morning. *"Mujhe waqt ka pata nahin chalta. Kabhi bhi uth kay sajde main gir jaati houn,"* Kalsoom replied.

Zubaida explained to her that *namaz* did not work that way, and said that she'd teach her to pray. She further learned that Kalsoom only repeated God's name and that she did not know how to *say* the *namaz*. Zubaida promised to teach her.

A month later, when Zubaida was teaching Kalsoom, little Yahya came and sat beside his mother. He wasn't so little anymore, and he could tell day from night and knew how to turn on the television.

"Mama, what are you doing?" he asked whilst offering his Super Crisps to his mother.

"*Beta*, I'm teaching Kalsoom *namaz*. When you grow older, I'll teach you too."

"What is Kalsoom?" he inquired with a mouth full of chips.

"Yahya, Kalsoom is *Maasi*'s name. Now don't ask more questions and let me teach."

Puzzled, little Yahya sat in silence, gobbling chip after chip, eyes widening with curiosity as he saw his mother talk to the living room wall. Yahya had seen her talking to herself before, but he had always thought that she was rehearsing her office work or talking on the phone. But now, Yahya knew that the office work was done on the laptop and that the phone needed to be next to one's ear to talk.

Years passed by, and Yahya started going to school. He realized that people talked to each other and not to the walls. He also could not make out what his mother wanted from him. When he walked to school alone, his mother did not bat an eye. On days when she did not have work, she walked him to school. When Yahya said that he had come from the school by himself, she threw a tantrum saying that unless Kalsoom came to pick him, he couldn't walk back from school. Yahya didn't know who Kalsoom was. But according to his mother, in the morning when he walked to school alone, Kalsoom walked with him.

When Yahya was six, he thought that Kalsoom was a feeling. When he was ten, he thought that Kalsoom was his mother's imaginary friend. When he was twelve, his friends called him the boy with the *pagal* ami. Yahya loved Zubaida. She was all that he had, but he also knew that she wasn't like other people–that she wasn't normal.

When Yahya graduated with a degree in psychology, Zubaida was overjoyed. She thought that all her hard work had paid off. She made sure that she brought Kalsoom to the graduation ceremony as well. Yahya had learned not to be embarrassed of his mother. In fact, he reserved two seats–one for his mother, and one for her Kalsoom. Two days after her son's graduation ceremony, Zubaida was in a car accident. She had run across the road from the street on her way back from work, tripping over one of the cracks she had stepped on, and had injured her head. She died right on the spot, under a broken street lamp post.

Yahya was deeply saddened by the loss of his one true love. He had wanted to treat her with love, to cure her of her dissociative identity disorder, but his mother was no more. A month after his mother's passing, Yahya woke up from his noon nap because of a rather familiar smell coming from the kitchen. The doors were locked from the inside. He went to the kitchen to see that daal was being prepared on the stove – Kalsoom's, daal that he had enjoyed growing up.

❻ – The Hospital

Dr. Sarmad wanted to run away. He was a twenty–eight–year–old married man with a three–canal house in Cantt, two cars that came with a driver at his disposal, a wife who made the perfect *aloo* gobi parathas, and a baby on the way. But Sarmad still wanted to walk out the door and never come back.

You see, Sarmad had not always been this way. There were days when he'd giggle sheepishly at the silliest of things, and when he'd video tape his entire day. He liked doing that–capturing moments, reliving stories, painting colors onto blank canvases. He liked talking to the camera, expressing his views about his next–door neighbor's dog, about how Valentine's shouldn't be haram, or how his mother got ready for her friends and not his father. He liked it very much.

On such days, he loved *maasi* Rubina's sugarless kheer, he adored dropping his brother to the Oasis resort which was on the other side of Lahore, and most importantly, he loved the idea of *shaadi.* But now, *maasi*'s kheer tasted like air, driving to the nearest park made him dizzy, and he wanted his wife to fall down the basement stairs and die.

"Grow out of it now, Sarmad. *Bohut hou gaya hai.* I will break your bones and your camera. Baba *kay* friends *ko* Mark Zinger burger *say zyaada pata hai.* Search *per aao zara tum,"* his parents insisted.

Dr. Sarmad closed his diary and turned on his phone. His parents' actions tasted like Toot Syah, awfully sweet to digest. His wife was no different.

"Kya camera *main* videos b*anane ka janoon hai. Bache ko* videos *baich kay parhao gay? Tauba hai, ami nay kaha tha* doctor *hai,* Saliha, doctor," she would say.

Sarmad didn't like cutting up people. He wanted to cut videos. He didn't like sewing them back up, either. He wanted to create content. He wanted to travel the world in anything but a white lab coat. To others, it was stupidity. It was *nashukrapun.* But to him, it was longing for a dream.

He scrolled down his screen, looking at videos of Irfan Junejo, the man he wanted to switch lives with. He laughed at his comments, he lived his daily routine and when Irfan got married, Dr. Sarmad wept outside the operation room with tears of happiness. He zoomed on his wife's photo.

MashaAllah. A woman who supports his talent. A woman who loves Irfan for who he is. A woman who lets him love the camera more.

He then kept the phone in his back pocket and returned to take check on his patients. With every step he took, he felt like he had the entire world settled on his shoulders. The halls suffocated him. He felt like the smiling nurses were laughing at his misery. He tried to smile back, but his lips were too dry to stretch.

One day, he got an email from Dr. Tariq, his father, living in Canada. He felt nauseated at how formal their relationship was. It was almost sickening how the letter was addressed as if it were sent to a fellow colleague and not his son, and how particular the font was.

Respected Dr. Sarmad Tariq,

This email is to inform you that a hospital in Sahiwal requires your immediate assistance. The information regarding the hospital; from its location to its urgent complications, has been attached.

You will be required to work in the hospital, for eleven months. After that, you'll be awarded a leave of 35 days.

If you choose not to go, after eleven months, another surgical internship will be offered and you can avail that to complete your program.

Regards,

Dr. Abdul Tariq

With dry, chapped lips, Sarmad beamed. He felt like this was the closest he would get to freedom, and so he decided that this would be it. He would pack his bags, serve at the hospital in Sahiwal, and once done, he'd have thirty–five days to disappear. This was his Willy Wonka golden ticket, an opportunity to run away, start a life and document it like Junejo. He would finally have a life worth living.

A week later, Sarmad was off to Sahiwal. It was a short drive, and he got out of the car a kilometer away from the hospital.

"Sorry, sir *jee*," the driver said. "It's almost Maghrib time. No one takes this road after Maghrib time."

Sarmad didn't ask why. The hospital was on the other side of that road, and he decided to drag his suitcase there. The trees were a darker shade of green on this side, and the ruthless wind tore the leaves off the branches. Sarmad picked up a leaf that landed on his leather shoe. *Kash camera hota. Itna khoobsurat hai yeh.*

Sarmad looked sideways before opening the camera application on his phone. He chuckled as he did so. There was no one but him, a tree trying to save its leaves, and the fierce wind. He tapped the screen several times before it focused on the leaf, and then he took a photo. Sarmad smiled.

He placed his luggage on the ground and extended his arm to make a video. His whole body was smiling at that point. *"Asalamolaikum nazreen! Aj hum majood hain* Sahiwal *main. Main apka manpasand* Sarmad *a.k.a* Samoo. *Mousam khushgawar hai aur us say bhi zyaada khushgawar hain hum!"*

Sarmad felt as if he was on cloud nine. With his now radiant face, he walked towards the hospital. During the walk, he snapped photos of the glimmering street lights, blue boards with arrows, and rusty old dustbins.

The hospital was much smaller than the one he worked at. The nurses did not smile, and the only thing the canteen served was a lunch box with Twist juice, a chicken patty, and a drumstick. And the drumstick was almost always undercooked. At night, Sarmad would take a stroll outside the guesthouse and eat khichri from a *dhabba.* Sarmad made friends with the owner.

"Bhai Sahab. Kuch hi loug iss side per raat gayay atay hain. Buche dophair ko hi khichri lay kar bhaag jate hain."

"Buchoun ki pitae karne wala hota hai na koyi ghar," Sarmad laughed, *"meri karne wala koyi nahin hai."*

The shopkeeper smirked. *"Phir bhi. Apki himmat hai."*

Sarmad was assigned to the psychiatric ward. With each patient that came and went, Sarmad's diary became heftier with notes and medical records. He had begun to like Sahiwal. It was the khichri and the odd cases that he adored.

Day 12

My patient today was a young girl. Her name is Sajida. Her parents say that she falls a lot, and does so *jaan booch kay.* Initially, they thought that she was clumsy or maybe her eyes were weak, and that glasses might help. But, she's ten and she jumps off the roof by herself. She bangs her head into a wall till blood oozes out from the space between her tiny eyes, and last week, she tried to set herself on fire.

When I talked to her, she said that someone pushes her. She stated that someone pushed her off the roof, someone threw the matchstick on her and someone banged her head on the wall. *"Dhum dhum karke marta hai dewar main mera sar. Main kehti please ruko per jo koyi bhi hai, marta rehta hai.* I simply went upstairs to call mummy *jee* and someone pushed me off the edge. *Kehta ab yaad kare gi tu kalma, ab khole gi tu* Quran." I believe that the girl was not lying. Her parents are awfully strict and religious, as a result of which she has internalized their narrative, creating an imaginary being. But in reality, it is just her subconscious causing her to harm herself.

Day 89

My patient today was a divorced woman who sewed her husband and children's lips shut. Her daughter reported that she gets these 'fits' in which her bones crack and she moans in pain. After that, she crawls on her legs, bent like a spider. She forgets to urinate in the bathroom, and says that a black woman with the same face as hers perhaps a doppelganger sits next to her at all times. *"Wou meri shakal ki hi hai.* Her tongue is like a serpent's. Her eyes are milk–white. She has horns too. At night, when I sleep, she comes and sits on me. *Mudham awaz main* Amnaaa... Amna utho... *bolti rehti hai. Meh kehti houn nae uthna tou moun chat'ti hai."* Upon being asked why she sewed her family's lips shut, she replied that she didn't want them to shout when they saw the other her. The other woman didn't like shouting. I believe that the woman has multiple personality disorder.

Day 202

Today, the girl from day 12 came back. She said the oddest things. I believe that she might be schizophrenic, but I still have to rule other illnesses out. She said and I quote, 'Today, I began praying. I always knew how to pray but I never actually prayed. At that moment, I heard a dog barking behind my house, almost as if cats were fighting and an animal was in pain. When I glanced towards my left shoulder at the end of *salah,* I saw a woman sitting near the door.

She extended her arm towards me all the way from there and pulled me towards her. Her lips didn't move, but I could hear her through her nostrils. She was looking at me as if she would eat me, her eyes popping out of her sockets."

I asked her what the woman said. *"Kehti aisay nae karte beta..aisay nae karte beta... aisay nae karte beta...* She kept repeating this until my eardrums hurt." I think the girl has created an imaginary figure to get out of praying.

Day 267

Today I was sent downstairs to the morgue to check on a corpse. It wasn't any ordinary corpse. It was the corpse of a woman who had died giving birth. According to the reports, it was decaying by the hour, and we had no explanations for such rapid decomposition. Her death had been reported in the early hours of the morning, and due to an unknown infection, bugs were eating out her right eye.

The strangest part was that even the senior–most doctors could not figure out why the insects feeding off of Yumna Jahangir were creepers that were only found in the soil of a certain place in Bangladesh when Yumna had never been. Eerily enough, the insects had been reported to be extinct. Yumna had actually been buried for three hours before the man working at the graveyard reported that an awful stench was coming from her grave. The doctor who checked her last said, *"Iske uper lanat pari huwi hai. Yeh zaroor kale ilm main mulawis thi."* Of course, that's none of our business. We need to see what's eating up Yumna from the inside, and if whatever it is has been transmitted to the baby.

Day 300

I checked the baby. She's beautiful. The staff named her Pakeeza. I think it's a beautiful name. Round face, bright brown eyes, and an adorable nose. The baby is well.

Dr. Sarmad wrote each case down in his journal and took photos using his phone. He planned to create a video documentary series out of this experience once he could leave Pakistan. He had it all jotted down; he would divorce his wife, tell his parents that he'd had enough, move to Canada till the visa was valid, and buy all the equipment he forever longed for. He had thirty–five days to turn his life around, and he could not wait. On nights when everything was a little too overwhelming, he'd have khichri and watch Junejo's web series. He was his own little Junejo in his mind.

As the eleventh month approached, he called his wife and told her that he was coming back. He couldn't reach her because she had been rushed to the hospital. The baby was almost due, but the labor pains had been false. Sarmad had not thought about what he'd do with the baby. The environment around him crushed dreams and planted toxicity, and fatherhood would not be possible. Maybe he'd meet the baby after a year or talk to the child through Skype. Sarmad eventually decided that he'd give his savings to the child and put the four homes that he owned in the baby's name.

Sarmad was told that his work at the hospital was exceptional and that his certificates would be shared shortly. Happy, Sarmad left for Lahore. He was greeted by his fleet of servants, warm *aloo* gobi parathas that he devoured with yogurt, and after eating, Sarmad slept. He woke up to his wife next to him. They had tea and discussed her pregnancy.

"When do you think the baby will come?" he asked her.

"Not any time soon, Sarmad. It's just been two months

yaar. Fake degree *hai* doctorate *ki?"* she replied.

Sarmad sat up and removed the sheets off of his wife. There was no baby bump. He placed his hand on the stomach. It was flat.

"Where's our baby?" he said in disbelief. His wife stared at Sarmad as if he were unhinged.

"Are you thickheaded? Seven months *baad aye ga na baby. Hadh hai,* Sarmad."

Sarmad looked at the clock; it struck thirteen. Had he slept straight through the night? He checked his phone. There were no emails or calls. He jumped off the water mattress and opened his journal. It was on the desk. There were no bags.

"Did you unpack my bags?" he asked her.

"Konse bags?"

His shirts were perfectly aligned in the cupboard, color coordinated by the servants. He opened his journals, and the last entry was his metaphorical musings regarding his parents' resemblance to panadol cough syrup. He checked the date. It was February 4th, the day he had left for Sahiwal. He checked his emails. None of the emails talked about the internship in Sahiwal. They were none from his father, and only one unread email regarding the shipment of the book Heer Ranjha from Daraz.

"Yeh kaisay possible *hai.* You *tou* believe me, *na?* I went to Sahiwal. For eleven months. I treated–I–I treated this girl. She's undergoing therapy–this woman–*wou apne ap*

ko sheeshay main dekh k ghabrati hai–I dissected a corpse… Haan Yumna, Yumna Jahangir!"

Sarmad's wife stared at him running around in circles, talking about a hospital and the patients he treated.

"What are you on about, Sarmad? You never got the internship. *Kaisi baatein kar rahe ho.* Which hospital? Which 35 vacation days?"

Sarmad banged his fist into the wall and told the driver to take out the car. He then drove to Sahiwal in his I love the moon' night–suit. He told the driver to stop in the middle of the road.

"Hum yahan say ageh chalain gay."

"Likun Sahab kyun?" the driver asked. Ignoring his question, Sarmad stepped out and began walking, followed by his driver. They walked and walked, and they kept on walking, but there was no hospital. *Idhar hi tou tha. Kahan gya.*

They went back to the car and drove around. There was no hospital–no khichri wala. They asked the people around. There weren't many, but the three they inquired about the details from said that there had been a hospital in the early 90s that had been burned to the ground, and the khichri *wala* Sarmad so fondly spoke about had died five years ago.

Sarmad opened his phone's gallery. There were images of him in his room, him holding a leaf in his garden, and that was it.

Seven months later, Sarmad and his wife and a beautiful baby daughter. Sarmad was sure that he had seen the child before. Round face, bright brown eyes, and an adorable nose.

❻ – Under Apa's Bed

On 18th May, a stormy day in 1995, multiple things were happening at the Atta's household. Dadi ama, also known as Begum Nasreen, was making moong daal without gas, on the cylinder. Her husband was having nightmares about his grandchild being born with carrots as eyes. Her *bahu,* Yasmeen was going into labor, and Mahnoor was desperately waiting for her baby sister to arrive by folding her pink quilts in messy bows.

The air was dense, and the clouds were moving around the sky in thunderous circles. The neighborhood cats were crying loudly at the same time, and it was almost melodious. The postman who lived near the Atta's was shutting his windows because *nachte huwe badal, roti huwi bilian* and the scent of undercooked daal signified the arrival of *sheytaan.* The postman, Mr. Suleman, whose name is not of any importance to this story, had seen similar signs in his *gaoun.* Furthermore, in his sixty years of life, he'd witnessed enough to know when the curtains needed to be drawn.

"Bachoun. Aj koyi bahir nahin jaye ga. Mousam iski ijazat nahin deta. Sakhti mehsoos hou rahi hai."

That day, Lahore's canal road was not graced by the

presence of men and children who had spent the previous afternoons dipping their bodies in the canal water. The water seemed to be in a rush to hide under the bridge. The Kalma Chowk signal, at that time a simple road without a name, had a hoarde of individuals raging at it, angrier than usual, honking like their lives depended on it.

It was summer time chaos, a scene out of a Spider Man coloring book, with drawings colored out of the lines borders by children who liked ripping the pages apart.

Convent's teachers let the students out earlier than usual. It wasn't a day to learn *alif bay pay.* It was a day to reach home before noon and sleep off the weariness. To buy oily samosas from the canteen's Abbas uncle because oddly, every child's lunch had gone bad.

And on that day, when the clocks struck eighteen, the Atta's welcomed a new family member. Yasmeen had her second baby girl, Begum Nasreen's daal finally softened, and her husband woke up from his recurring sleep terrors. Mahnoor waited at the door for her sister's arrival.

They didn't know what to call the baby. It was so big. She was so big. And she was getting bigger by the minute. She felt heavier after weeks, and carrying her became a chore Begum Nasreen couldn't do, and Yasmeen despised doing. The baby's grandfather coughed every time she was near him, and when the baby stared at him with her tiny, partially open, raven–black eyes, he felt like a carrot was stuck in his throat.

Mahnoor called her *apa,* because you call big people *apa* or *baji,* and her little sister soon outgrew her. Apa didn't eat or talk much, she just grew. Her face was plumper than a ras gullah's, and when she turned eight, she could fit into her ami's clothes.

Apa was intelligent. She could read everything with letters on it, be it Begum Nasreen's prescription, or Raaja Gidh in her grandfather's library. She could help Yasmeen with the *doodh wale ka hisaab kitaab,* and she could sketch faces better than she could remember them. But, no one liked apa except Mahnoor.

Begum Nasreen knew that it was because of apa that no one visited them; she was *bebarkati.* The *muhale walian* felt that someone stripped them off their tongues when they tried to read the Quran in that house, and so, the weekly bayan came to an end. The *doodh wala* no longer sent his son to deliver the milk, which meant that Begum Nasreen's house received milk only once a week, when the *doodh wala* came with the *doodh* himself. He said that his son's eyes went upwards and wouldn't shut each time apa had come to receive the milk.

"Meray betay ki binae jati jati reh gae. Sufaid hou jati thein ankein. Ghoom jati thein aur band nahin hotein thein. Tarapta tha jab tak darood parh kar nahin phoonkte they. Baba *ray* baba, baji *apki nawasi per asaib hai. Churail kahein ki,"* he said while shaking his head.

Yasmeen did not like her *beti* due to many reasons she

could not decipher. For one, apa had sucked her milk so much in the early stages that her breasts had fallen to her knees, and the doctors had no cure for that. Every time she tried to love her daughter's existence, bile rose up to her throat. It was like adoring an alien object. She had also seen apa pass through the kitchen walls, and those bricks were later covered with mold. It was as if her *beti* had created a disastrous world of her own where no other life could exist for long.

"Isay kisi aalim k paas lay kar jayein," the postman, Mr. Suleman, advised Yasmeen one night. The next day, when Yasmeen had visited the postman's house, she had found his family grieving over his dead body. But it was no ordinary dead body.

There was dried urine on his Friday *namaz* clothes. The cracked bones in his unresponsive fingers were evident as they hung lifelessly. His nails looked like they had been bitten off by an animal. The corpse appeared to be freezing cold. It was the first time Yasmeen had seen a dead person so up close. Mr. Suleman's ears had to be covered with a velvet cloth; his daughters had reported hearing giggles coming from their father's ears, calling out to them. Yasmeen could not forget the feet. The feet had been stapled sideways. The ankles were broken, and the skin on the left foot's pinky toe had been scraped off.

The following night, Mahnoor had reported Mr. Suleman's voice coming from apa's room. "Ama, I heard them having a friendly conversation. They were talking about boiling carrots."

Begum Nasreen's husband, Zafar–ud–Din, was petrified of his granddaughter. He walked around the house with a pocket Quran in his *kameez* and often tried not to offer his prayers in the house. During the nights, when Begum's husband saw apa shaping her body into a bridge and walking on her arms and legs with her head upside down from his half–shut door, he covered his eyes with his wrinkled hands. It was fast, apa's crawling, and sometimes, she'd stop and turn towards her dada abu's room. Zafar–ud–Din would think that his heart would plop right out of his chest and he'd lose consciousness. He'd murmur the *Pehla Kalma* under his breath and refuse to open his eyes until he'd hear the national anthem being sung after the morning bells at the nearby street school.

Mahnoor liked her apa. She'd teach her the numbers, and how there was much more in this world than what met the eye. Every night, apa would read paragraphs from Frances Hodgson Burnett's *A Little Princess,* translate them into Urdu, and tell Mahnoor about Sarah Crewe, the girl who could imagine things.

"She needs the attic and loneliness to meet her saviors. All we need is to get under my bed," apa would say.

And so, Mahnoor and apa would lay down under apa's bed, and nothing would happen, at least not for Mahnoor. She would just get a rash from the unwashed carpet on her neck and arms. Apa, on the other hand, would talk, laugh, shout, and cry under the bed. To Mahnoor, it merely looked like apa was talking to the wood above them.

One fine afternoon, when the house smelled like mattar qeema, and the windows let fresh air circle the corridors of the Atta's house, Yasmeen sat in their little garden, oiling Mahnoor's short, wavy hair with yogurt, oil, and egg. Sitting under the warmth of the August *dhoop,* feeling her ami's fingers pull through the strands of her tangled hair, with yogurt dripping down Mahnoor's dimpled chin, Mahnoor decided to tell her mother about what happened under apa's bed.

Yasmeen, curious to find out more, told Begum Nasreen about her new finding. "Yasmeen *teri bachi manhoos hai.* Mahnoor *ko us say dour rakha kar,"* was her response.

The following evening, when apa had gone with Mahnoor to play in the park opposite their house, Yasmeen entered apa's room. She hadn't entered it in months. She always wanted to send the *maasi* to clean it, but she knew that the *maasi* worked in all other houses in the neighbourhood, and if something strange happened, everyone would know about her troubled daughter. The room seemed to lack air. Yasmeen opened the windows and the washroom door. She then rolled her body under the bed and closed her eyes.

For the first minute, it was nothing but her thoughts, a few tears of sadness regarding what her life had become without her husband, and the thought of having made a mistake by giving the *darzi* an advance.

In the second minute, Yasmeen started to feel pleasured. She began to feel her body lift itself in the air, as if resting on petals of *gende ke phool.* With her eyes closed, under apa's bed, she felt an uncontainable adrenal rush course through her body. It was almost like the last bite of a Wall's Cornetto, a crunch, and the chocolate melting on the top of her tongue–like the feeling of a new Chen One bed–sheet on an old bed, like holding Mahnoor in her arms for the first time, like a cotton bud in her ears rotating itself whilst hitting the sweet spot, like *maasi* Hafeeza digging her fingers into her chest after a shoulder massage on a sunny Sunday.

Yasmeen was transported into a room with a yellowish light, the kind in movies during flashback scenes. The room was different from any other that she had seen. Maybe it wasn't so different, but the walls were not familiar. She could smell the fresh paint off them. It was a small room, but it fit many people happy people, women dressed in cotton frocks and green stockings, in long, buttoned–down gowns and white hats with polka dots, and jolly men with tucked–in shirts and folded brown pants. Her body felt content. It felt like she was in an English school that she couldn't go to when she had been younger like she was in Europe and she could finally have fresh puff pastries, the shape of eclairs, which tasted like *shakkar* and happy memories. She walked around the room and saw Mr. Suleman, smiling and reading the newspaper. He looked at Yasmeen and chuckled. Yasmeen spotted Major Yaqoob, and suddenly, she felt like the whole room stopped to look at them.

"Ap yahan hain? Apko pata hai apke begair main kesay waqt guzarti houn?"

"Pata hai mujhe, jaan."

Yasmeen hugged her husband under the yellow lights and wept in his arms. He looked like he had never left her. His smooth, military shaven skin brushed against Yasmeen's. They had tea together. It was *elaichi* tea with extra *jhaag,* just like they both adored it, in fancy cups she had seen at Al–Fatah three days ago.

Yasmeen woke up and saw the wood above her. Her body felt heavy again, and beneath her, she felt the carpet prick her. She had been robbed of her husband's presence and the uncanny warmth. She was once again under her daughter's bed. Yasmeen sighed. It had been a beautiful daydream.

She closed her eyes once more, in attempts to escape back into the world where she was married, where she could drink in cups she longed for, with English music in the background, with a smiling man on the piano, ladies with satin aprons serving *khajoor* like toffees, and where Mr. Suleman hadn't died that godforsaken death.

This time, however, Yasmeen just felt something wet touch on her arm. She opened her eyes and turned her head sideways. She gasped in fright and banged her head on the underside of the bed. Groaning in pain, she slithered towards the bedroom door. Yasmeen had seen a little blue boy, drenched in water, with hollow eye sockets, lic*ki*ng her arm.

Sundays at the Atta's were more sorrowful than usual. Yasmeen was looking at her *shaadi* album with salty tears sliding down her cheeks; Mahnoor was trying to understand why Tom couldn't catch Jerry after so many tries; Zafar–ud–Din *Sahab* had a bad cough attack, Begum Nasreen's face had swollen due to an allergic reaction, and cold, sores covered her body. Apa was not around.

The bell rang and the cuckoo of the electronic bird echoed in the house. No one was expecting anyone. Mahnoor opened the door to the familiar *doodh wala* and an elderly man standing next to him. The milkman had brought with him a friend.

"Mujhe yakeen tha kay apke ghar kay halaat theek nahin hain. Zulfiqar *Sahab bohut phonche huwe aalim hain. Siraf* Quran *aur sunnat say ilaaj karte hain. Meray gaoun main aye they aik bachi per say saya utarne tou socha unhe yahan lay aaoun."*

Zulfiqar *Sahab* was indeed a pious man. Even before entering the house, he had sensed unearthly presences. He showed himself around the house and then sat down near Begum Nasreen.

"Iss ghar main jinnoun ki basti rehti hai. Sab bure nahin likun sab ache bhi nahin hai. Ap apni beti ko bulaein."

Yasmeen fetched apa from her room. Apa refused to walk down the stairs. Instead, she stood on the top most step, staring at Zulfiqar *Sahab*. She kept twitching her nose and breathing heavily.

"Fikar na karo, Joseph. Main tumhe kuch nahin keh raha. Main bus jannna chahta houn kay bachpan say tumhara khandaan iss bachi kay saath koun hai."

Apa sat on the stairs and started to mutter words under her breath. Her speech was incoherent. She then stopped, and ran back to her room.

"Jab ap," Zulfiqar *Sahab* said, looking at Yasmeen, "pregnant *thein tou ap shayad* Murree *gayi thein. Apka teesra maheena tha. Jharioun main apne peshab kiya tha.* Wou aik Christian *jinn kay buche per tha. Us din say unhoun nay apni aik basti apki beti saath rehne kay liye bhej di."* Saying this, Zulfiqar *Sahab* took his leave with the milkman.

"Main apki koyi madad nahin kar sakta. Likun Multan *main aik alim hain jou apko is mushqil say nikaal sakte hain. Baaji, go to him. Take your family along. InshAllah, sab theek hou jaye ga."*

But before Begum Nasreen and her family could plan to visit Multan, Yasmeen decided against it. She realized that she wanted to spend her days under apa's bed. She wanted time with her husband in the bedroom which was always sunny. Joseph could manipulate her world for her.

And so, she stapled Mahnoor, Begum Nasreen and Zafar–ud–Din's eyes shut. She made them lie under apa's bed. She didn't want them to see the blue jinns, all she wanted them to see could be seen with eyes shut. Zafar–ud–

Din passed away in his sleep that night, Mahnoor didn't see anything, for she had gotten *azaan* recited in her ears when she had been born, not once but multiple times, and Begum Nasreen was reduced to an illness that left her bedridden. Yasmeen, on the other hand, grew very fond of apa. Both of them slept under the bed, and visited the sunny room every morning, noon and night. It was a blissful yet a terribly, terribly addictive dream.

Chapter 5

Nae Naweili Dulhan

Majid licked his ten–rupee Jetsport like his life depended on it. He stood under the ruthless sun and its scorching heat, sucking the artificial flavor out of the molded ice. The streets of Lahore were empty at noon. The year was 1989; it was the first of Ramadan, and Majid had decided not to fast because today was the day he had been waiting for all his life–it was his *baraat.* His driver instructed him to throw away the popsicle, for the color of the sticky syrup would linger around his prominent lips.

"Bhai, shaadi per tou rang barange hount ache nahin lagte na."

Mian Majid smirked and continued to let his tongue play with the tip of the ice–cream. A thin line of sweet sweat trickled down his chest from the corner of his mouth.

Majid belonged to a traditional family in Hasipur. He had lived there amongst his *barey* for twenty years. Their village was rich in heritage and culture. The women of the house made delectable achaar which was shipped to the city every week. However, their family was spat upon. They were illiterate beings, with power, money and loaded guns. Most of the women in the house had come in as young girls, stripped apart from the families in neighboring villages; the others had been *ki*dnapped from under the city lights because of their enchanting beauty. Majid's wife to be was no exception.

Earlier that month, when Majid had been traveling to deal with National Foods, a company which bought the pickle mixture from Majid's family farms, he had spotted a young woman getting out of her car on his way to their head office. Majid had seen women of all shapes and sizes around the world. He had visualized them in all forms, salivated from his thoughts, and rented films and ladies both on such nights. But, the woman he saw step out of the car made Mian's stomach churn.

She had defined features: an oval face, a caramel complexion, just like Majid's favorite childhood Spacer toffee, eyes the size of night stars, lips outlined bright orange, and a smile that made his toes tingle. She wasn't thin, but she wasn't fat either, and her hair was loosely tied in a bun. In her hand she held a notepad or a file, Majid could not really make out what it was, but it was shrouded in a shiny purple material - the color of Dairy Milk wrappers.

Majid instructed his driver to follow the woman to her office, and then to her house. He spent the day driving in circles, living the life of Rehmat Sohail, imagining her wearing his mother's wedding clothes. He took pictures from a digital camera and called his father to make the necessary preparations, for he would be bringing home his wife.

There was another rule in Mian's family, which Majid was quite proud of. Before having things done their way, they did it society's way. And so, with jeeps packed with Saffron Crocus, the costliest flowers Majid could find, and baskets filled with Dubai's finest flavors of Cadbury Dairy Milk, Majid went to her house. The house was situated in Model Town, and it was the only house in that specific street. The flowers Majid had brought wilted at the sight of it, drooping to the ground, and Majid's dog began to bark. Majid called his dog Chotu, since it was smaller than the other dogs he owned and that day, because of his uncalled–for barking, Chotu was shot and thrown in the plot near Rehmat's house.

Mian's family made their way inside. It hadn't rained in days, but the walls were wet, and so was the furniture inside the house. It was moist and damp. A woman hesitantly led them in after seeing the guns.

"Ap koun hain?" A child asked as Mian stepped inside. *"Ap yahan kyun aye hain?"* Mian handed him a chocolate and told him to scamper off.

The boy took the chocolate and asked each member of the family the same question. *"Ap koun hain? Ap yahan kyun aye hain?"*

A woman carrying a wooden tray that held mini–sized

glasses of juice walked in, and she was accompanied by Rehmat.

Mian explained how he had seen Rehmat and how he had been left awe–struck by her beauty, mesmerized the very first time she spoke. He promised her the world–jewels from unheard of countries, clothes from the finest tailors, and achaar that would spice up her life.

The woman smiled, and so did Rehmat. The wedding date was set, and the *dulhan*–to–be shyly went back to her room.

"Ap na koyi pipe shipe theek karein ghar kay. Ajeeb ghar hai. Geela sa," Mian's mother suggested on her way out. Majid had, of course, not noticed for he had been very much in love.

The wedding took place with lots of glamor. The festivities went on for a month. Gold from the finest jewelry shops in Pakistan was showered upon the guests.

The first time Majid touched his wife, her skin appeared to be wet, as if her hand was placed under running water. The first time they made love, Majid thought that he was drowning in the tubewell in his gaoun.

Very soon, the walls of his house began to leak water. The drinks that were spilled in the house could not be cleaned. Clothes fell short of absorbing the liquid. The water did not evaporate. Cooking became a problem, and cleaning became a hassle. The children of the house always had runny noses and teary eyes, and no medication seemed to be curing them. At Maghrib time, the showers and the faucets in the washroom would rotate open, and water would mysteriously start to pour.

Majid's grandmother sat in the upper–most room of the house and started her *parhai.* She was fond of the dark arts. She had started with an *ustaad* and *wazifae* twelve years ago, and now, she had with herself a baby jinn who took the form of a young boy. She sent the boy to find out what was wrong with their house.

The boy went through the walls and returned in the blink of an eye, with a companion. The grandmother asked the jinn who the familiar face was, for she had seen her jinn's companion somewhere.

The young guest, the size of a gnome with completely creaseless skin, colored eyes and horns said that he was an Ifrit, a community of jinns that could be conjured. He told the woman that a *churail* lived in their house, and hence the house was slowly decaying. They said that the *churail* was a three–hundred year old *makhlooq* from the depths of the ocean. It lived with humans, for it was gifted as the *jahez* for a girl born to a necromancer. Now that the girl was dead, it roamed freely.

The grandmother, stunned, asked her jinn who his friend was. The Ifrit said that it was the same boy she had seen in the witch's house when she had first gone there. A lot of them were settled there. *"Ap koun hain. Ap kyun aye hain?"* he had said.

The grandmother remembered, and all the pieces fell into place. She decided to get rid of the sorceress. She sat for thirty days, feeding on anything but meat, reading dark, satanic verses, trying to conjure Majid's wife. Rehmat was an ancient creature, and so, she was powerful. She disrupted the circle of the elderly woman's chants, and the old woman bled from every hole in her body till she died.

A year later, Majid stumbled across his grandmother's findings whilst renovating the upper–portion of the house to sell it to an Afghan man who wished to turn it into a restaurant. Majid had become a weakling and had lost most of his hair. He now carried with himself a pack of tissues because he sweat excessively.

The man who was standing there looking at the shelves of his restaurant being installed, told Majid that he had dealt with such entities. The only way to get rid of this one was to die it out or dry it out. *Die it out or dry it out.*

Majid did not know what this meant. He knew that slowly, he was dying. His family was dying. His appetite was dying. His sleep was dying.

For the first time in his life, Mian had started praying. It hurt, for every time he went into *sujood*, he felt that his wife was wrapped around his shoulders.

And so, one morning, when Rehmat got up and left the room, Mian noticed something that had been in front of his eyes all along. He noticed that his mattress was damp, and the place where Rehmat slept was soaking wet. He remembered seeing the wetness since the day they had gotten married. He got up and dragged the mattress to the roof. He placed it under the sun to dry.

He went down the stairs, and saw Rehmat staring at him, whispering to herself. The whispers that came from her body sounded like multiple men talking in a small room.

Allah hu Akbar. Majid knelt and recited the little part of the Quran that he had memorized. He felt a bolt of lightning shoot up his veins. The little boy from Rehmat's house stood next to him, biting his neck and arm.

But Majid stood there till the mattress dried and Rehmat vanished. He then collapsed and breathed his last breath, but he felt dry, drier than a dessert, like a hair dryer was blowing in his face. He felt the scorching heat of the day in Lahore. He felt warm. *Die it out or dry it out.*

And so, with the last drop of liquid that evaporated from the mattress, the walls of the Mian's house stood stronger than ever, and the fungus in the jars of achaar disappeared.

Chapter 6

Chachu Ali's Jinni

There are tales of love and of lust, and then there are tales of longing, yearning, and remembering. This is one such tale in which no matter how many sleeping pills and *duaein* Ali drowned in himself, in his finest sleep, his eyes remained open, and his memory stark. He searched the pale white walls of his brother's house for a glimpse of his love.

Mariam looked at her chacha browsing through the Sunday newspaper. He s*ki*mmed through the comics, paused at the cricket section and, as always, bit his lower lip when he got to the *purasrar waqiyat* column. When Mariam had been young and gullible, chacha had fed her stories of *pichal–peris, dayans,* and women with sweet–toned voices who hung from *banyan* trees.

In her childhood, Mariam had been fascinated by such creatures, but now, she just felt sad for her chacha. She had spent years listening to his narrations with anticipation in her eyes, Thinking that one day, she'd meet her majestic chachy who belonged to the world of jinns, but that day had not come.

Her ami, who had been reluctant to tell Mariam how she felt about her husband's brother, now strictly forbade her from spending afternoons with chacha Ali.

"He's not well," she'd *say* to Mariam whilst tightening her hair in a ponytail. "We thought that he'd grow up, marry, and work at your papa's office–but he's stuck. In a world of his own. And I don't want you listening to his nonsense anymore."

So, Mariam tried her best to avoid Ali chacha–the man who ate porridge and drew pictures of pale corpses with hollow eyes all day long. Eventually, Mariam got married to a friend, and on the day of her wedding, she wanted to tell chacha Ali how much she needed him to let it go. She wanted to speak about heartbreak and loss and moving on, but her chacha just smiled when she sent him a Chicken Soup book, and he smiled again when she joked about her husband's available chachy. And the entire time, Mariam wondered if chacha was, after all, not a gloomy man drenched in sorrows, but mentally challenged.

Two days after her *shaadi*, Mariam found herself missing her chacha more than she missed her parents. She felt angry at him for not being normal, but most importantly, she felt that she had to see him. It had just dawned upon her that they did not live under the same roof anymore. Her *nand* drew women too, but those were just the Power Puff girls from Google images.

Her parent's house was quieter than usual, and she spotted her chacha sitting in the lounge, peacefully sipping some kehwa. His round face was deprived of *noor*, and the chin on his skin hung loosely–like a sack of grain. His uncombed hair was gelled back with coconut oil, the smell of which was more overpowering than the *elaichi chai.* Mariam nestled herself on the sofa next to him, and in the comfortable silence between them, she started to observe the fading *henna* designs on her sweaty hands.

"Chacha," she said, after a long wait. "What happened to you?"

Ali looked up and rubbed his eyes. It seemed as if this whole time, he had not felt Mariam's presence. "What happened to me?" he repeated her words, in astonishment. "Does the coconut oil make my forehead look bigger?"

"No, it's–"

"My forehead is so big that Malik Riaz could buy property on it," he cut in with a joke.

Mariam smiled uncomfortably. She wanted to get up and leave. But for the first time in a decade, she stayed.

"Why are you like this? Why are you so obsessed with jinns and witches? Why did you ruin my childhood by telling me that your wife is a *pichal–peri?* Why–"

"My wife *is* a *pichal–peri,"* he answered calmly, noticing that the conversation had taken a turn.

"See, this is exactly what I am talking about. You've made this make–believe world of your own and you don't know what's real anymore. The doctors say that you're perfectly normal–then why are you punishing yourself and papa?"

"No one's standing in the corner. No one's punished."

Mariam sighed. "You're punishing me," she whispered under her breath.

She wondered if her chacha was the reason she had studied psychology in the first place. She wondered if psychology was even a subject because, unlike God, no one could really decipher the depths of someone's mind. Her thoughts quickly drifted to the shaljam gosht her *saas* was cooking, and without much ado, she asked her chacha if he'd like to drive to the roundabout to have some cheese shawarmas with her.

Ali nodded and even though he wasn't hungry, he didn't want to disappoint Mariam twice in a row. His mind was preoccupied, but he did understand emotions and people, and he wished that his family knew that. He wished that Mariam knew that.

As artificially flavored cheese dripped down Ali's beard, he looked at Mariam gobbling down her last bite. He put aside his half–eaten treat and wiped his sticky hands with tissues.

"What's wrong?" Mariam asked, not surprised. "Won't you finish your food? I told you to have the one without cheese, chacha."

Ali shook his head. "It's not that," he replied. "I want you to know what happened."

Mariam looked at her chacha, clearly very surprised. She told herself to not get excited because, in the end, chacha could be resorting to the two things he did best, cracking political jokes or going on about things that made little sense.

"Drive around in circles," he continued. "I want to feel as if the time has stopped. You won't feel dizzy. I will tell you what happened thirty years back. But, it is important that you keep on driving round and round so that I um–"

Mariam didn't question him. She didn't mind if she looked like a lunatic driving around the roundabout until Ali chachu's tale ended. This was the closest she had gotten to having a serious conversation with him. And so, they drove in circles while he finished his story.

"I was twenty years old. Or maybe a few years older, I don't remember. But, I was trying to grow a beard. I was the only friend who didn't have any facial hair, and that irked me. So perhaps, I was nineteen. I was studying business – I was good at supply chain management, so good that I got an internship in the first year of business school. But, I wasn't the parhako type – the type people pick on. I wasn't popular either, but we had a decent group. Please don't mind if I add in unnecessary details. It's just how I remember the story. There was a girl in the group named Alina. We liked each other – Alina and I. She went beetroot red around me, and I liked the floral scent that she wore. Your dada abu got us engaged at the end of our second year. It was like a typical relationship, and we were in love, or at least I thought so. *Phool shool thay, band baja tha*–you know, we were happy souls incredibly attached, fascinated by the idea of togetherness–"

Mariam started to picture a hyper chachu, surrounded by lights and a silver *sherwani*. Her young chachu, with the walls of his room empty, – not yet covered in portraits of supernatural entities, folded at the edges, smudged with coconut oil–his now dusty shelf clean, with shiny business books on top. *He always was a good storyteller,* she thought.

"Alina used to make this milk dessert. She'd just mix three things and pretend that she'd made a Master Chef dish and she'd laugh in a carefree manner– with Rafhan's jelly falling from the space between her front teeth. Everything was real, like today's newspaper and us driving in circles, very real. But, I just remember bits and pieces of it, and that is fine. For the real story begins after that."

Mariam wanted to stop the car, but she was afraid that he would stop narrating, and that years of her thinking about why he was the way he was would have amounted to nothing. She did not want that.

"My friends and I, without the girls, decided to go on a trip to Murree. Just us boys sneaking out to the mountains to enjoy some sheesha and games of *rang.* That's what we really did. Yawar had membership at PC, but none of us wanted to drive to Bhurban. We wanted one room for eight boys, and a restaurant that served daal chawal stored in hotpots from days ago. We wanted an adventure. I remember telling myself that I would welcome Murree's breeze with open arms and reflect on life. And that's what I did. It was a happening trip; I still remember the color of the clouds that visited us through the open window whilst we slept on top of each other, the stolen Peshawari *chappal* that I picked up from a stand, the echoing screams of the monkey Yawar was running away from, Zain's magical camera which made us look the size of mountains, and the quilts that, to this day, we still think had bedbugs. I remember it all.

The morning before our checkout, I scampered off alone down the uneven road, puffing a mint–flavored cigarette. It was pitch black, and each step felt like a jump off the cliff. I don't know how far I had come, but the whispering wind was awfully inviting at that late hour, little whispers and small hugs – *thandi hawa kay jhonkay.* Very soon, I realized that I was walking towards a blurry blob of light. The closer I went, the shinier it became. I stopped when the sound of my footsteps was synced by an instrumental sound – to be precise, the *chun chun* of *payal. Chun. Chun. Chun.* I won't lie; nothing seemed amusing about the weather anymore. I felt scared, sweaty, and the wind had started to blow in the opposite direction. I wanted to turn back, but somehow those peshawari *chappals* suggested otherwise.

Within a minute, the blob of light that I had been

advancing towards most unwittingly, turned into a rusty lantern held by a woman your age. She held the lantern close to her milk–white face – the color of Alina's desserts. Her nose was pierced both ways, and her blue eyes were coated in *kajal,* giving away her Pashtun ethnicity. She smiled, and a dimple formed under her cheeks, and I caught myself thinking, if she looks this bewitching in the darkness, how spell–binding would she be when light surrounds her. It was then, or maybe a minute later, that I noticed what all travelers in Urdu digests do the pretty woman's feet. I couldn't see them. The light showed bony legs and ankles covered with anklets but no feet. Nervously, I moved forward which most travelers from Urdu digests do not do and saw that her feet were backwards, twisted. She was a monstrosity from Hindu dramas. I thought that if I ran, she would run after me, with her twisted feet and the lantern the size of her face. The faster I would run, the faster she would get, and so, I decided to hold my breath. I do not know when I lost consciousness. The aftermath of the winter drizzle made the muddy soil collecting on the roads smell like my apartment's closet."

I wanted to believe that Chacha Ali was narrating the truth, *kyun kay* most of what he was saying sounded like what he read in the mornings with *chai,* but the expressions on his face were unsettling, and I felt that I could make a few more rounds without getting dizzy.

I woke up after what seemed like a stressful sleep, but in fact, I had just been unconscious for a few minutes. As I opened my eyes, I saw the same unearthly eyes staring at me, and I gasped in horror and stood right up. My legs felt wobbly, and I realized that I had been resting in her lap. The sky was a shade of lavender, and the air rushed past us carrying a fresh smell. I was not in Murree. The woman, with her mouth shut tight, in the most melodious voice, told me that she was a *pichal–peri,* the daughter of a practicing Muslim jinn, and that she meant no harm. Again, Mariam, her mouth was shut, and the voice came from her nostrils, which expanded and relaxed, mirroring a butterfly's movement. I asked her where I was, and she said that I was where I had always been, on the rocky mountainous road of Murree, except that now I was seeing their world because she wished for it to be seen. I asked her what time it was, and she said that time had stopped, just like it does when we move around in circles, and everything seems like a whirl – our thoughts and our body. I remember that I saw an unattractive blue colored child with white eyes and a bloated stomach walking towards me. She opened her mouth, and showed the jinn child her snake–like tongue before it could reach me. The Jinni then held my hand, her fingers locked into mine like milk and honey, and on her back, I flew across the sky.

I flew across worlds. I woke up on the cold road, with Yawar throwing energy juice at my face, surrounded by the others. At once, I looked for the woman I had seen, and I saw her - I really did, with her blob of light – moving behind the shadows of dawn. I pointed at her, I told the others to look, I begged them to stop her, but they saw nothing, and I started crying, in fear and pain. They brought me back, and I was never the same again. I spent weeks in my room, calling out to her, I went back to Murree and slept on that road again, but she never came. I held Alina's hand, and pressed her fingers against mine, but they didn't mix like warm milk and honey, and nothing in my life made sense anymore. It was like I had swum in a river of grape juice and all I could now see was water.

Chacha Ali looked up and told Mariam not to stop driving the car. He told her to be calm and not to panic and of course, she didn't because she was driving past the same gol gappa stand she had driven past for the last hour, but chacha gasped at the sight of it, and tears ran down his lifeless cheeks. "There she is."

Chapter 7

Blue Khussas

1989

Rimsha Mehmood–ur–Rehman, daughter of Shameem and Shah Mehmood–ur–Rehman, carefully placed herself behind her new bhabhi's old bedroom door. The match between Australia and Pakistan was being aired on a box–like thing called the television. The new bhabhi, who came from the family of Murree Brewery manufacturers, had brought this luxury item for the ameer with her, and it had taken Rimsha's entire *khandaan* by storm. Aunties, uncles and even *dour ki* Parveen Baji was talking about it. *"Shamo ki bahu* pass color *wala* tv–set *hai."*

Rimsha was fond of two things; *khussas* and cricket. On *chaand raat,* the women of the house would wrap themselves in colorful veils *abaya*s adorned with laces, pearls, and traces of celebration, and accompanied by the men, they would shop for shoes. Rimsha's favorite kind were Multani *khussas* – also known as *mojari* in her family. She could tell the solid material from the copy just by examining the footwear by hand.

She was also the only woman in the family who could decipher cricket. None of the women were inclined to learn about a men's game. When she was two, her birth ami Abida bibi had passed away due to an unknown cause, and before her abu had married Shameem ami, Rimsha had been fed, put to sleep, and even bathed around radio shows discussing cricket. And so, she understood the glory of the ball, the bat, and the player.

Rimsha's bhabhi, Falak, was an intelligent and cunning woman. She would often invite her sister–in–law to see recorded matches on her magic box, and when the delighted Rimsha would squeal in joy and leave the room, Falak would tell everyone about how much of an unsophisticated, *ghar na bananay wali larki* Rimsha was.

When Eid approached, Falak made up her mind to get the most beautifully crafted, canvas printed, snug fit for her precious feet. She frowned upon the women who told her to let her *nund* choose for her. She made sure to enter each shop before Rimsha did, seductively unwrapping her *chaddar* in front of the shopkeepers and laughing at each thing they said. *"Apna best* piece *dekhaein. Jou kisi aur pass na ho,"* she'd say.

One by one, they went through all the shops the fancy ones with huge billboards, and the smaller ones near the chowk. But, Falak couldn't find a single pair of shoes which outshone Rimsha's picks for the three Eid days. At one point, she thought that she'd get the exact same ones, but it wouldn't be the same as getting better ones. The women of the house were getting tired and were contemplating going home, when across the street, something caught Falak's eye. Next to a woman in shabby clothes, who appeared to be a beggar fast asleep on the footpath, were glittering blue *khussas*. They were wrapped in a silver foil–like sheet, and only the front of each shoe was visible. *Yeh jootay iske tou hou nahin sakte. Someone must have dropped them.*

Falak quietly excused herself from the crowd of women and went towards the mysterious shoes. The closer she went, the brighter they shone. It wasn't the moon light; it was the gem–work on the shoes– stones brighter than any she had ever laid her eyes on. *They have to be real stones. Just look at them sparkle!*

Falak looked sideways and then slid her feet in the *khussas*. Little chum chums inside her belly churned with happiness. Not only were the *khussas* exceptionally beautiful, they were also a perfect fit. She felt as if God had wanted her to find these – as if whoever made and left these, did so especially for her.

The women of the house gathered around the living room's wooden table to show – off their alluring shoes. Rimsha's dadi, the head of the house, sat in between them, examining and approving their choices. When Falak took out her *khussas*, dadi's jaw dropped in awe. All the other women found themselves to be inclined towards the *khussas* well. Nothing that pretty had been worn by any of them before. Since the dadi liked the shoes so much, one of the women suggested that she should have them, out of respect. Falak felt her face boil with anger. She nodded hesitantly, but the moment the servants came in with the tea, Falak vanished with her shoes.

The next day, Falak dolled up in a bright orange *jora* which had been sent to her by her ami, stitched by the finest craftsmen in Karachi, with the most delicate sea blue outline on the edges. And yet, it was her *khussas* which transformed her into a desi Disney princess. The day was filled with praises about the noor on her face and the stir that the shoes caused. Falak felt like the television set sitting in her room – luxurious.

As soon as the day ended, Falak started to feel dizzy. Her head hurt, and she had trouble walking down the staircase. Seeing this, dadi called Rimsha and asked her to call Ahmad Shah, their occasional cook, and tell him to cook gulab jamun in the back kitchen. *"Khush khabri hai, oye. Umeed say hai* Mehak–ul–Falak!"

The mithae was sent, the announcement was made a week after and the doctor was called home. On inspection, it was found out that Falak was not pregnant, and that the dadi had been mistaken. No one, including Falak's *mian jee,* wanted to go to Falak's room. They also believed that she had faked 'an *awazaar tabiyat*' for attention. Days passed and Falak did not come out of her room.

Dadi told her son that not only was Falak a jhooti aurat, but she was most probably, involved with other men.

"Talaq dou usay!"

"Likun ami kyun? Kamray main chup chaap pari rehti hai. Subah jis huliye main chor kay jata houn wesay hi hoti hai."

The dadi brought in the postman, the cook, and the *safai wali,* all of whom claimed to have seen Falak roaming the streets after Maghrib in the past couple of days.

"Bhai Sahab. Falak bibi *ko apni gunagaar ankhoun say dekha hai. Parde kay begair. Laal* lipstick main."

"Chup kar jao!"

Furious, Falak's husband stormed back to his room. He was a wise man who handled his abu's office operations. And so, he had been taught patience. Instead of talking to his wife, he decided to lock her inside the next day.

He would store food for her and lock the door–*kundi bhi aur taala bhi.*

What bothered him more was his *biwi's* sudden silence. She no longer demanded money, told him tales about how her baba *jani* always pampered her, or how they should move to a separate *haveli.* In fact, she hardly talked. Her eyes appeared lifeless, and it was he who forced her to change clothes. The only time she smiled was when they made love.

He liked Falak this way. Though mildly bothered, his mind was at peace. He believed that she was repenting for the drama she had put up earlier. One night, on his way home, a member of his society's party asked him to join him for some *chai* at Pearl Continental. Both he and Rizwan Akhtar sat in the lobby, sipping hot tea.

"Ap kou shaid meri baat naguzar guzre Farooq *Sahab. Likun sab baat kar rahein hain.* Mehmood *Sahab meray bohut azeez hain. Izzat ka sawal hai."*

"Kehiye Rizwan. *Kya baat hai? Ap ka rang fak hai. Kya koyi pareshani wali baat hai?"*

"Baat darasal pareshani wali hi hai likun btate huwe dikut mehsoos ho rahi hai."

"Please. *Ap kehiye."*

What Mr. Rizwan said next, left Farooq Mehmood–ur–Rehman's throat dry. He had just been told that his wife appeared in other people's houses at night and, for lack of a better way of putting it, "Put up a show no *khandaan*i woman would."

There was no doubt in Mr. Rizwan's or the others' minds what they had witnessed. All of their wives recognized Falak, and the whole society, if not the whole town, was talking about Falak and her *laal hount.*

Upon reaching home, without any *salam* or *dua*, which was very much frowned upon in the Mehmood household, Farooq went straight to his room. Falak sat there, expressionless as ever, staring at the wall. Her skin was paler than usual and she was trying to murmur something under her breath. Once he got closer, Farooq noticed that the bedsheet was covered in menstrual blood, both dry and wet, dripping from between Falak's legs. Near the bed were Falak's blue *khussas*, covered in mud.

So, she has been escaping from behind locked doors. I have married filth. I have married a street woman.

And right at that moment, Farooq ordered Falak to leave. He divorced her – not out of anger, but out of pure disgust. And, when Falak made no sign of movement, Farooq picked her up, put her on his back – she felt heavier than usual–and attempted to throw her out of the room. In the process of doing so, he looked at the mirror placed between the bed and the dressing table. He saw that on his back was no Falak, but a woman in his former wife's clothes, with eyes the size of wrists, and long strands of hair which were thick and rough like an old *banyan* tree's roots, wrinkled *baasi tamatar*–like skin, and a smile that showed no teeth.

The woman wrapped her arms around Farooq's neck, and her twisted, backward feet around his waist, licking Farooq's left eyeball. Her tongue was glued to his socket, and as he yelled in pain, he threw the inhuman creature across the room. The woman squeaked, carried the *khussas* in her mouth, and on four legs, went through the wall.

Later on, Farooq was charged for the first–degree murder of his wife, Falak, when her body was discovered inside her room. It displayed an injury on her head that had resulted from being dragged across the bed, allegedly, of course.

Chapter 8

Rehmat ka Ghar

2009

Aunty Tehmina wasn't an average fifty–year old Lahori woman. She was a women's rights activist, and she hated how she needed to cover her sagging parts with chiffon *dupatta*s. She thought that she wasn't too old to have milae parathas for breakfast, and that she certainly could drive to the *ki*tty parties held at Mall 1. Back when Tehmina was twelve, and her skin wasn't *khajoor* like, someone had told her that she looked like Tehmina Durrani. Tehmina believed that it wasn't a coincidence that she had the same name and that she went to the Convent of Jesus and Mary. Later on, Tehmina got married to one of her abu's colleagues who was fourteen years older, and in all terms, a gentleman. Rabnawaz didn't smoke, he took young Tehmina to the cinema for the first time, got her a pet poodle from his army friend, and at night, he'd press his head close to Tehmina's and tell her tales of his mining adventures in Peshawar. Till then, both Tehmina and her life was rather ordinary.

But when extraordinary things happen in ordinary lives, it is important to list out the little details. Six months after aunty Tehmina's marriage, Rabnawaz went to get milk and did not come back. His clothes were there, the smell of the *itar* he wore was still in the bathroom, and his Boski *shalwar* suit was neatly hung outside their bedroom door. The only two things missing from the house were packs of Nestlé Milk, and well, Rabnawaz himself.

At first, the parous wale thought that Rabnawaz went out of the city. Then they started to talk about his second wife. Tehmina was not impacted by *lougoun ki baatein*, but she thought of all the times she had fought with Nawaz and started to believe that he might just have had enough.

"People snap, right Tipu?" The only being that Tehmina talked to was her pet dog, who too seemed to have a long, oval chapatti like face since his master's phantom–like disappearance. "Do you think the other woman has crooked teeth like mine? He always liked my vampire teeth. I can chew so many *reorian* at once."

Bills started to pile up and Tehmina began to teach the neighborhood children English Literature. She only got twenty–thousand, but with her savings, it was enough for her and Tipu.

Months passed, and unusual occurrences made their way

into teacher Tehmina's life. She started dreaming of stairs – never ending ones. She'd wake up with aching legs–as if she had carried an *attay ki bori* for long summer hours. After each dream, her belly button would get terribly itchy.

One night, she decided to inspect it – her belly button. She couldn't see anything, so she put the tip of her index finger inside; it felt hollow, like the middle of a donut. Slowly, she put her entire finger inside. It slid in like it had been laced with ghee. The ghee Rabnawaz never washed off his fingers. Her belly button stretched to make room for her hand. Horrified, she took her hand out. The tingling feeling returned, and winged ants started to fall out of it. Some flew, but dozens fell on the ground, their wings coated in ghee.

But, that wasn't all. Tipu fell sick. He would bark day and night and gradually, he died. But his barks remained in the walls of the house. The rooms were never silent. Aunty Tehmina – thirty year old Tehmina – decided to move out at that point.

It's the house. Rabnawaz's house. It's weeping. Gum main hai. I need to leave the house. Rehmat nahin is ghar main.

Since Tehmina was a little girl, she had always come first in debates. It wasn't because she was very knowledgeable, it was only because she argued her way to the win. Years later, she used this skill to make her friend, Iffat, hand over her empty house in Defence. Iffat had moved to Dubai, and her house in Pakistan had no *kiraedar*. And Tehmina had always wanted to live in a posh area, where McDonald's reached the door hot, where Sundays could be spent roaming around Bareeze with other *khawateen*, whose biggest issue in life would be matching their *joras* and sandals. The thought of a new house made her want a new husband, someone who preferably didn't drink milk.

I'll start looking for one once this iddat shiddat time period is over, you know.

Fourteen years passed in that house. There was a specific room Tehmina couldn't sleep in, a rat infestation in one of the bathrooms, and occasionally, she'd have pleasurable dreams that'd make her feel young. It was during the fifteenth year, that Tehmina started to see things. Little women, dressed in Sindhi clothes, dancing to the rhythm of their heartbeats. And Tehmina would dance with them.

When she'd feel ill and the medicines wouldn't work, she'd read the Quran and beg Him for forgiveness. And on days when she'd forget to read it, she'd play it on speaker loudly in the house and she'd feel better.

In August of the year 2009, Rabnawaz Ikram buried his wife Tehmina Rabnawaz, who died during a ruqya–an Islamic exorcism being performed on her.

The story that you've read? That is Tehmina's life through her eyes under the influence of black magic and the multiple jinns who had situated themselves in her body. Her daily collections of notes show that Rabnawaz was erased from her memory twenty–seven years ago. They also have a child, Ahmed. Tehmina used to carry him on her back. But when asked, she said that she had a monk sitting on her shoulders with his skinny, yellow legs hanging down her breasts. They thought it was schizophrenia, but a mental illness doesn't allow you to levitate in the air, crawl on buildings, and be found in some Iffat Maqbool's house every night, which is at a two–hour distance.

Chapter 9

Jurwa Behnain

2019

In ancient times, twins were considered to be a bad omen. Mothers would throw the second baby delivered into the sea, and would watch it drown. To the ami, it was not a child, but the devil that had been born with her off–spring.

Somewhere in the world, in the early 16th century, amis who gave birth to twins were burned alive. They were thought to have had sex with shayateen.

Then, there was an era when twins became acceptable, for science called them two halves of the same person. During that time, Greek mythology was fondly read, and people believed that twins possessed special powers.

Twenty years ago, when two girls were born in the Butt family, the whole town was lit up with *shaadi* lights, and ras gullay dipped in sweetened milk were distributed among the family members. One was called Noor because her face shone even at night, and her eyes were brighter than the moon on *chaand raat.* The other was called Areeba because she seemed at peace, and when Noor wept out of hunger, Areeba remained quiet, for she knew that she'd be fed. And so, she was Areeba, the wise one.

With both heads wrapped in their dado's crimson and lilac *chaddar,* which smelled like a closed room and festive *phewian,* the twins would creep outside of the house on summer afternoons. The winter fabric that kept dadi's body warm after *wudhu* made the twins sweat profoundly, but it was long enough to cover them both. So, with bent heads, they'd lean against the corroded gate, waiting for the Walls ice–cream man to paddle by. Noor would pick a lemon popsicle. Later, when her lips would turn a shade of yellow, she'd pretend to be sick and sit in her room, memorizing Urdu poetry. Areeba would always buy two feasts, and under her dadi's *chaddar,* she'd take both the lollies to the rooftop and share them with Zum Zum.

Areeba didn't know what fascinated her more–the sound of the chocolate nuts being crushed under her teeth, or watching a little girl that only she saw, wrapping her snake like tongue around the ice–cream.

Zum Zum wasn't someone special. Areeba had always had 'imaginary' friends according to her family. There was a time when Areeba spent hours explaining to Noor what the boy who slept between them looked like, or how he smelled like mangoes and couldn't see. But Noor would always go back to playing with her Barbies.

"He has buttons for eyes. You fight with me when your *guriyan* go missing. You look everywhere for them. But I can see him gamboling with them. I don't tell you so that you don't snatch them from him. He won't like that. He says I'm his *gurriya* too."

But Noor, since childhood, would roll her eyes and pay no heed. She adored her sister, of course. They both relished biryani and home-made pancakes, and art made out of expired crayons. And yet, Noor never knew what Areeba had talked about her whole life. Zum Zum, dispenser *main rehnay wala aadmi, ulte paoun wala* painter, *phanke say latki huwi chambeli* – the list went on.

It had started with a *maasi* who cleaned Areeba's mess, braided her hair, and got her colorful bunties. She'd lay next to Areeba, combing her hair with long, fleshy fingers, telling her about lands where jinns roamed. Her voice would ring in Areeba's ears, and eventually caused her to get her period years before her sister, Noor. Areeba understood that what she had was special, but when she reached grade seven and learned painting aesthetic navy blue waves on her ami's vases, she realized that her ability to see the unseen was both a talent and a curse.

In the January of 2019, the sisters were traveling to the northern areas. To Noor, the sky wept at the sight of her, the mountains chanted *Lab per aa ti hai dua bun kay,* on the top of their rocky voices, and the little pebbles that got stuck in her sneakers meant good luck. To Areeba, the *veyraan illake,* simply meant more entities. She despised the thought of Murree, for in the vehicle, from one window she'd see the sun setting, and from the other, she'd see the late hours of the horrendous, windy night storms. Noor would comment on how the car slipping through the snow was a metaphor for her relationship with her dada, but Areeba would see the truth; a long–legged bent man with one eye on his forehead, pushing the car down the road.

But January is a month of happening things. It's a promising start, a long mahina, and just when Areeba was gleeful to have landed back on the sand grains of Karachi, something peculiar happened. The events that followed seem like a blur, perhaps because of their nature, but they made Noor believe in something more than her city's calling and men's tears.

Sweetly tormented by their love for branded ice–lollies at an aesthetic hangout after art school, the twins ended up at their *manpasand* popsicle shop. Areeba sat on the corner table, playfully sucking the flavorless stick. With sticky fingers, she sheepishly blinked at her sister to let her have a bite of the frozen lychee dessert. Just then, like one of those Tom Cruise movies, a soft breeze knocked Areeba's *dupatta* off her head. *That's odd. The door is closed.*

The wind blew again, harder this time, like a soft whisper turning into a shrieking scream. And that was enough for

Areeba to realize that there was someone else except the aside from twins on that very table.

The twins' ami always used to tell them that, "*Beta*, when guests have a portion of your food, there's no *hisaab* for it on the Day of Judgement." Areeba had always thought that maybe that was the reason she fondly accepted uninvited beings to be a part of her life, every day.

She looked over her shoulder and saw that a dwarf *aurat* sat next to Noor, slowly licking her ice–cream. "*Yaar* Areeba. *Aj* ice–lolly *theek nahin bani.* Forun *melt ho rahi hai.*"

She thought that the thing, like all the others, would leave. But, the little lady with aluminum gray, popped open eyes, kept staring at Noor. And just like that, it followed them back home. Areeba knew that it could sense her ability to see her, but even then, it made no contact. It followed Noor to the washroom and came back bigger. And when Noor knelt down for *sujood* at Maghrib time, the jinni sat on her shoulders.

Days passed and Noor started to fall ill. It wasn't the type of sickness that their family doctor Kamil *sahab* could treat. For when Noor complained about sleep paralysis, Areeba saw the creature with its glittering *dailay,* standing on Noor's chest, and its five thumbs, trying to make its way into Noor's nose.

Areeba wished that she could yell at it, and she even did– but it made no difference. She replaced Zayn Malik's DVD and played *ayaat* on their portable speaker, and temporarily, the being moaned and left. But the next morning, it'd be there–closer to Noor than before, almost as if it *was* Noor.

Areeba asked her father if she could visit her neighbor whose children were taught by the local mosque's *qari sahab*. She insisted that it must be done for a project and so, she went to talk to him about her sister.

"I believe it's my fault. I attract these things. But they've never shown themselves to Noor. And now she's slowly being drained out of life. She says that her rice taste like cardboard."

"Beti, tell your abu and then bring her to me."

And so, hesitantly, Areeba told her abu *jaan* about Zam Zam and all her friends. *"Na manein ap, likun wou tou scholar hain.* Taking her to such a learned man will do no harm."

Noor, feverish, refused to move from her bed. Her once rosy cheeks that almost narrated tales of sadness, looked like an aam without *gutli* – lifeless. The *qari,* upon entering the room, smiled and sat the family down.

"There's nothing to worry about. *Saya nahin hai. Sheytani bhi nahin hai. Jinn hai. Likun* there are no signs of possession. In fact, *Noor* has one of their possessions. Once she returns it, they will be on their way."

"Likun, hum kesay pata lagaein?" Areeba asked.

"Main baat karta houn." The *molvi* hummed and sat with his legs crossed on dadi's red shawl that once served as an escape cape. Areeba saw that the entity spoke in an unknown language, with its mouth closed. The others just got goosebumps looking at Noor's unpleasant *halat.*

Slowly, it pointed at Noor's *jhumkas,* and the *qari* instructed Areeba to take them off of her sister's ears and throw them out of the window. As soon as she did, the overgrown elf figure went through the wall, like evaporating vapor from ami's biryani.

Noor designed those jhumkay herself ... Likun iss per tou moti lagae they wou Murree ki sarak say uthae they. Jinnoun ka tabar wahan say baraat lay kar guzar raha tha.

That night, Areeba sat on the sofa, having refrigerated lychee, telling Noor all that she had seen in life without an Instagram filter.

Chapter 10

The Hungry Jinns

❶

Caramel sponges drenched in sticky butterscotch syrup, wrapped in whipped cream and topped with edible floral roses that tasted like marshmallow fluff and ami's warmth in the winter days. Zainab looked at her creation. The cake stood still in all its glory, and she let out a content sigh of relief. The clock was striking thirteen and Khadim Zubair had already packed the fondant. Zainab did not choose to work at night, but it was the only time during which she could give birth to her scrumptious children, the only time she could bathe them in warm milk and the only time the images of her recent divorce would not rewind and play repeatedly in her mind – like the snow–covered trees in the rearview mirror that follow you no matter how fast you accelerate on the Nathiagali roads.

Every time she turned off the kitchen light, her body felt at ease. The switch was associated with her body, and when the switch turned off, she felt her muscles relax, for they had been granted permission to drift into a much - needed slumber. The following day was a challenging one because Aunty Parveen's daughter Yumna, was getting married, and Zainab had to make her wedding cake. Zainab had opted for a traditional cake with mint green icing to go with the bride's *lehnga*, but Yumna had insisted that the cake be grand, taller than her husband, broader than the fragile table that had to carry it, four-tiered, because otherwise, it would just be – well, – an ordinary cake.

Zainab's morning was spent assembling the layers of red–velvet batter, and her evening was spent mixing the cream–cheese. The cream cheese had to be heavy, heavier than the dowry that her former husband had asked for, and creamier than the *mithaas* that covered his lies. At night, Khadim said that her kitchen was too cramped for the fondant to be rolled and placed on the cake. He insisted that the decoration procedure be carried outside the kitchen, on the utensil shelf. Zainab thought that the racket might wake up the neighbors but Khadim assured her that it wouldn't. She was tired and did not want to spend the remaining hours looking at Khadim's bony fingers skillfully rolling fondant, so she nodded.

She realized that if she shifted the work outside at night,

her khala's *maasi* next door would take care of any excess mess. And so, every night till Fajar prayer, Zainab would work in the open air, making sweet delights to sell and cooking steak to take for lunch to the office the next day. Her khala said that one should not cook at night, one should not turn the stove on at night, and one should certainly not roast meat in the middle of the night. She had no reason for saying what she said, and so, Zainab paid little heed to it.

A week later, Zainab decided to switch up her steak recipe. Initially, she had started taking it for lunch because her colleague at Nestle had suggested that it helps to lose weight. But now, it wasn't fulfilling. In fact, no matter how much Zainab marinated it with spices and *adrak* and *lehsun* paste, the chicken would be tasteless. Browsing through the internet for ideas, she came across an appealing recipe which seemed to resemble that of Howdy's mushroom steak. Zainab was pleased. Like all good things that come to an end, this chicken quickly lost its charm. Somehow, it started tasting bland. Zainab's khala stated that it was because she cooked in the late hours of the night.

On one such night, when Khadim had stored the fondant back in the fridge, and Zainab was grilling chicken and frozen vegetables, she heard a humming sound. It was a low hum, the kind that a flute would make, but not quite because it ended on a shrill note. After a couple of minutes, when Zainab turned off the flame and the sizzling of the chicken came to a halt, the hum was heard again, and it seemed to be coming from behind the wall at the back of the stove. Zainab walked to the end of the *gali,* and saw that behind the old stoves sat a little boy. He was barefoot and his face was dirty. His complexion was dark, and his oily skin shone in the dim light. His eyes were peculiar because they glowed like a cat's.

"*Tum* khala Iffat *kay ghar kaam karte ho?*" The boy shook his head.

"*Andar kesay aye ho?*" Zainab inquired. The boy pointed towards the pan and Zainab figured that he must be hungry. Since her khala's gate, the one that divided her house from hers was wide open, Zainab assumed that the boy was the new errand- keeper khala had kept to fetch her medicines from the Pharmacy.

Before Zainab could move and offer him some leftover cake, the boy walked towards the pan and uncovered it. With his bare hands, he took the boiling hot chicken out and sniffed it. He smelled it like he was devouring it, and then, quite suddenly, kept it back and started to walk away. Zainab, who was already both angry and troubled, felt sick to her stomach when the boy, like a ray of light, passed through her – from within her body – and disappeared in the darkness.

Zainab ran to her khala's house. She ran as fast as her shaking legs in her tight chooridar pajamas would take her. She started to wail, and wiped the soft tears of fright from her *dupatta*, and for about an hour, she lay next to her khala without saying a word regarding what had happened. When she finally narrated the event, her khala brushed away the sweat, and told her to perform *wudhu* and go to sleep.

In the morning, Zainab was told that she had fed a *chalawa* (jinn)'s child. The smell of meat and sweets before Fajar invited the unseen to her house. The jinns fed upon the food being cooked under the stars, and it was because of that that the food had lost its taste.

Awais did not like his ami *kay haath kay khanay.* In fact, he despised them. It wasn't always like this. There were times when he yearned for her tinday, Friday's *daegi* style biryani, white karahi – everything his mother made in the early days. He wasn't *nashukra;* it was just that he got addicted to ordering food online. And since his ami loved his plump cheeks that lifted with joy when she handed five hundred–rupee notes to her son, she did not mind waking up to empty Hot and Spicy paratha roll boxes in the morning. In Awais' household, important things were discussed at the breakfast table. Important things such as raising taxes, future education, Aunty Sanila *kay betay kay* grades, and why brown bread was better than white bread.

Ghosts had never been a topic of discussion. In fact, Awais himself doubted their existence. When his bhabhi had implied that at birth, she had seen a man sitting on her shoulders in the bathroom, Awais had chuckled with delight. He then had quoted a pregnancy fact relating to hormones. When the house help had asked *baji jee* for extra leaves because her daughter was levitating in the air, Awais had instructed the *maasi* to not wed her daughter against her wishes.

"There's no such thing as jinn *bhoot,* only logic," Awais would say to his sixteen–year–old puberty–stricken LGS girlfriend. "The time you spend developing ghost busting apps, put that much effort in scoring for your SAT, *yaar*."

It was one such usual night when Awais was sitting on his bed, munching a poorly assembled burger from the one place that delivered at five in the morning. Awais decided that he would order Bundu Khan's poori halwa platter for breakfast. He took out a five hundred rupee note from his ami's bag, and placed it under his pillow. When it was time to order, he took out the money and found out that he was holding two five–hundred–rupee notes. Awais smiled and kept the second note in his pocket.

The next night, Awais put the money on the shelf, next to his Aloe Vera gel, and started to practice mathematical tests online. When it was time to order, instead of the three hundred–rupee notes that he had kept, he found that there were six such notes. He went out to see if his mother was behind the doubling of the money, but the doors were locked, and abu's snoring could be heard from upstairs.

Several nights passed, and each time, his money would

be doubled. He spent one night staring at the notes and yet, in front of his very eyes, the amount got doubled. There was no logical explanation for it, but Awais kept enjoying the extra amount of cash. Surprisingly, this 'doubling' would only happen in his room, at midnight after the lights would go off.

A month later, whilst playing PubG with his mouth full of chatni, Awais received a tight slap across his face which threw him off the bed. A chunk of mint chatni fell out of his mouth, and his cheek swelled up to the size of a congratulatory laddu. The lights in the living room were still turned off, and no one was in sight. He had been smacked on the cheek by an invisible hand in thin air. Petrified, with a blotch of urine on his shorts, Awais ran to the nearest room, which was his bhabhi's.

For a week, the lad was bedridden and had a high temperature. He missed his SAT exam, and though the doctors said that it was stress, bhabhi *jee* called the local *qari sahab* from the mosque to examine her brother–in–law. On inspection, they found out that friendly Hindu jinn, who was around a hundred years old, was briefly residing in Awais' room whilst traveling across Pakistan.

He had been increasing the amount of money that Awais used for ordering food so that Awais would order some for him. When Awais didn't order food for days on end and ignored the whispers in his ear by increasing the volume of Michael Jackson songs, he got hit out of 'playful anger' for not being a good *mehmaan.* Before the *molvi* could communicate more with the jinn, it left. A few days later, the *maasi*, whilst sweeping under Awais' bed, found a packet of Haldiram nimko–from India.

Chapter 11

Part me, part jinn

The wind was blustering. The sky was weeping. Some said it was tears of happiness and others sobbed in agony with it. A dog and its pups were getting drenched. Their fur was weighing them down so that their bodies were barely off the ground, like cotton buds soaked to the core, and their eyes were blinded by nature's dust storm. A man threw a cardboard box from his apartment on the fifth floor and ran back inside to close the windows on the unwelcome weather. The book was torn from the right side, with a picture of a TLC television screen, the 2019 model. It landed across the road and caught the dog's attention. I think the dog was called Tipu.

He looked like papa's friend, Tipu. I am not insulting Tipu uncle; he was a nice man who lived a nice life. But, just like the unmoving dog and his shivering pups, Tipu uncle drenched himself in sorrows till he got external help. And just like Tipu *sahib,* the dog *knew* that his shelter would come. I saw the dog carry its pups to their new cardboard home. The process took fifteen minutes. I wonder how it chose which pup to carry first. The dark one with a white blotch under its drooping ear was taken last, and was almost unconscious, ruthless raindrops piercing through its fleecy skin. Life's like that. Unfair. I feel like I am Tipu, the horrid rain, and the last pup – all at once.

Jan 8th, 2019

Papa thinks a lot. I think a lot. But, he says that my Thinking is different. It is meaningless. He has traveled the world and he speaks fondly of his experiences. He says that I have only one experience to speak of. But, he does not understand that my experience is more happening than hundreds of his. He sits on the table and stares at the *aloo*s floating in the shorba. He frowns, and decides to eat onions soaked in vinegar instead. I look at him in disgust. He is trying to become someone he is not. He thinks he is the Malaysian man who gave him a ride in his car, the British woman who handed him a biscuit, and the European man who drew a painting of him. But, he is just papa.

Jan 9th, 2019

We used to have an Apple TV before we moved to Lahore. There were three things that I loved about it. One, when I would be reading Archie comics before my exam, the shiny black screen would show ama's reflection moving towards my room from the corner, giving me exactly ten seconds to hide the comic. Two, if I focused hard enough, I would see a Japanese woman with one breast and white eyes sitting inside the screen. Her golden hair and her jaw dropped till her nipple. Sometimes she'd be sitting and other times she'd be walking with her head dangling sideways like a partially cut *kharbooza* waiting to break free and fall. Third, whatever I would draw on my iPad would appear on the Apple Tv. Sometimes, it would malfunction at night. I'd hear, *"Kya dekha tha us din?"* in my ear in a soft, soothing voice. *"Kya dekha tha us din?"* and I'd wake up in the morning with the same thing written on the television screen. *"KYA DEKHA THA US DIN?"*

Jan 10th, 2019.

I have studied psychology. I know who Sigmund Freud is. I know that when you experience something traumatizing, your brain can act in an unnatural manner. You can hallucinate, you can get petrified, and even a bowl of noodles can trigger your mind. Papa says that I need to let it go. Papa does not like me sitting with aunty Galia and phupho Shameem. I speak of the yellow in the walls, the cavities that dentist drills out, what eyeballs taste like and I speak about *that* experience. It is raining again today. Not fiercely, though. *Sakoon wali.* I can smell the soil. I can feel the earthworms crawling out of the mud and I want to put salt on them. They wriggle–they tremble when you sprinkle *namak* on them. Little threads of protein with spice. I want to put them in my mouth and taste their grubby meat – specks of mud, the sticky exterior, the fleshy interior, and Shan *ka namak.*

Jan 11th, 2019

I wasn't much of a thinker. As a child, I thought that Thinking would shrink my brain and that my brain would melt out of my nostrils. I didn't think when I booked the ticket to Karachi to spend some time with my khala, and I didn't think when I decided to help the fifteen–year–old boy on the plane. But after *that* experience, I started thinking. I think about the warmth of the urine dripping between my legs in bed. It is magic. I feel ticklish and happy and warm and comforted, and when the warmth passes, I feel cold and wet and exposed and raw. I think about Tooba's misshapen lips. Papa doesn't have such lips. Mama doesn't have such lips. Such lips need to be fixed. I think about putting Vaseline on them. Ensuring they attain the moisture they need. Biting them. But eventually letting go. I think about poking them with a pin and injecting them with the shreds of a local lip pencil. I think about them being a bride's lips. I think about sewing them together like a beautiful piece of knitted art.

people were asleep as it was past midnight, and the woman next to me had slept too. The lad did not look normal. I mean, he was dressed well but he looked like he was mentally ill because he kept gazing at me and lic*ki*ng his upper lip. I was uncomfortable.

The moment I'd stop making eye contact, I'd hear my name again, and it would be a long, soft whisper which would travel through my body and make my hair stand. Shortly afterward, an uncle came and took the boy away. He caught me looking and smiled apologetically. I was sleep–deprived. I wanted to sleep before I could hear my name again. I tried sleeping and dreaming about the spicy mutton my khaloo would barbeque for me in Karachi. Tender pieces marinated with sweat and *masala.* I wondered if I could eat raw mutton. The thought was fairly disturbing at that time and I started to play Flappy Bird on my phone. From the corner of my eye, I felt a shadow pass my seat quickly.

It happened numerous times until I caught a glimpse of the same boy running past me. Except, he was only running in one direction – he'd vanish through the curtains in front and reappear from the curtains in the back. The woman seated next to me woke up and went to the back – I assumed she went to use the loo because she borrowed some of my wet wipes. *I must have been dreaming or something,* I thought. I rubbed my eyes, stretched my legs, and relaxed. I wished that papa could have sent me in Business Class.

Just as I was about to close my eyes for the seventh time

that night, in an attempt to sleep, I felt an eerie sensation – the scary feeling students get when they're from conservative brown families and it is Result Day the following morning – that type of feeling. I opened my eyes to find the boy sitting next to me, staring at my chest. I will not lie, I do have big breasts–the size that makes my mother frown because unmarried women aren't supposed to carry huge racks, the size that never lets papa let me leave my room without being gift wrapped in a *dupatta*. Before I could tell the boy to go back to his seat, I realized that he was glaring at the gold Allah necklace that dada abu had given me when I was seven.

"Kya phenti rehti ho, Zoya? Utaro isay beti," came my dada abu's voice from the young boy's body.

Jan 13th, 2019

Before I continue my story, I would like to talk about two things, my day, and the story of how I got the gold necklace. My day was fine. I felt irritated at Fajar time and I deliberately did not pray. I haven't been feeling like myself and I think that if God wanted me to pray, he would have made this sick feeling in my stomach pass. When I heard the *azaan,* I did not feel the peace I always do, and I did not cover my head. Each time the *molvi* paused, I wanted it to be over. Does that make me a *kaafir?* I do not think so. The odor of Yumna baji's French toast made me feel even sicker. I fried sausages and ate them. Meat needs meat. I sat in a corner the entire day, twitching and puking. Papa says that we'll go to the doctor tomorrow, but I am afraid that this is something that the doctor cannot fix.

But papa says that I am being dramatic. He preferring a lousy salad over aloo gosht is dramatic. When I was seven years old, I fell very ill. There are three versions to this little tale – the version that I've been fed by papa, the version that I remember, and the truth. I do not trust papa, and I do not know the truth, so I will tell you what I can remember. I went to the park with my maid – *maasi* Bilo at that time. She was a corpulent woman who kept her phone in her bra, and when someone called, she spent minutes with her hand inside her chest, trying to get the vibrating phone out. I think that she secretly liked it– fiddling with her assets. I also think that she is now dead. Anyway, we used to live in a joint family back then, so when my taya abu's children used to take Quran lessons from the *qari,* I used to join them. I was a great student.

I memorized Surahs and I recited them in the most melodious voice. Tayi hated that I got all the attention. *Maasi* Bilo and I were at the park that day and I was reciting my Surahs to her when the Walls ice–cream cartman entered the lane. All the children ran towards him, and I made *maasi* Bilo run to buy me a cornetto cup. Those were the good days – Walls was the best, and cornetto used to come in a cup. I was watching the children attack the ice–cream man like a swarm of bees. A man who smelled like fresh blossoms and whose feet were not touching the ground as he walked, came towards me. I remember that he was walking on air and that each time I sniffed, he smelled of pleasant things. He told me that I had a beautiful voice, and that I was gifted.

He said that the *qari* who taught me taught his children in the late hours of the night, but none of them were as good as I was. I smiled, and he smiled back. I asked him why he wasn't wearing any shoes and how come his feet weren't brushing against the wet grass. He said that he was a jinn, and that I had the ability to see jinns. He then offered me a funny looking thing. He said that it was a fruit from a far–away land, and it would taste sweeter than my ice–cream. I took the fruit, and, before I could thank him, he vanished. I ate the fruit and each bite of it tasted like a happy memory, like warm milk in bed, a fresh breeze, and like walking without touching the ground. After that day I never could have a cornetto. It started tasting like water. A week following the event, something strange happened. My nana abu and dada abu were cousins, so all of us lived in the same house.

My nana abu adored cats and we had several stray cats residing in our house. Nana abu would throw leftover gosht for them to eat. At night, I tip–toed out of the kitchen door, for some reason. I saw that, bent in an inhuman manner, gobbling the cat's gosht, was a black figure with bright yellow eyes and scaly skin. I screamed and fainted. I remember seeing such figures for weeks till someone told my dada that I could see the unseen. I couldn't see them all, just the ones that shape shifted – that weren't energies. To prevent something sinister being attracted to me, dada jaan had a necklace made especially for me, with 'Allah' engraved on it. The only time I took it off was when I showered and that too, when I had memorized the *dua* for the loo. Nothing interesting happened after that.

Jan 14th, 2019

I am afraid that I haven't completed my story yet – the experience with the boy – the experience that has altered me as a person. You see, with every passing day, I am losing interest in existing. My head hurts, and I hear and see things. For days, I kept Thinking that the geyser wasn't working, because each time I bathed, the warm water ran out. Last night, I saw the faucet move with my very own eyes from the red bar to the blue one. I calmly moved it towards the hot direction. For a moment, it stayed, but then someone – or something moved it towards the cold water again, roughly this time. I cannot hear the sound of prayer. I feel like grinding my teeth and shoving Johnson and Johnson's cotton buds into my ears till my eardrums rupture. Papa says that it is nothing. I say that he is foolish. I think that I saw dada abu in my dream. I saw him falling down a series of endless stairs.

Jan 15th, 2019

I will complete the story even though I do not feel like writing. I feel like there is something inside of me, spreading like an ink stain on a white uniform. I feel that you ought to know about *the experience:* Where was I? Ah yes the young boy told me to remove the chain from my neck. While he was looking at me, with his gigantic, bloodshot eyes, I felt that time stood still. Nothing but the sound of my beating heart could be heard. I felt that he could hear it too. I did not move, and the gold chain slowly slid off my neck and fell onto my lap. The boy smiled. *"Mera naam* Radhika *hai,"* he said. *"Tumhara naam* Zoya *hai."*

I felt myself freezing. It wasn't fear that held me captive, but an unknown force. I felt like the plane was stuck in a cloud, and I was stuck in a dream. From a distance, I heard footsteps approaching, and the uncle who I had seen before appeared with a *tasbih* in his hands and grabbed the boy from the collar. The boy yelped in agony as the beads of the *tasbih* touched his skin.

"Please," I said, *"Inke saath kya masla hai?"* The uncle looked at me with the boy's head firmly tucked under his armpit.

"Saaya hai iss per, bhen," he said. "We were instructed by a *molvi* to make sure he travels over sea so that the *bhootni* in him lets him be."

Saying so, the uncle dragged the boy to the back and right after, the woman sitting next to me came and sat back in her seat. "Thanks for the tissues. I always forget to bring mine."

Jan 16th, 2019

The truth is that I feel I have brought Radhika with me. I don't have dada abu to take me to a spiritual healer anymore and papa thinks that I need to bury my head in my medical books. It is as simple as that. I do not feel sick anymore. It started with anger–sudden changes in my behavior and *Astagfirullah* urges, then came the sickness – the feeling of being infested, and now, I just feel frightened scared of being alone and sleeping alone. I have read the previous entries in my journal and I do not recall feeling what I have stated. I feel like I am so many people at once.

Jan 17th, 2019

Today, I looked up ways to perform *ruqyah,* the Islamic way of cleansing. I locked the door, wanting to recite Surahs, but my lips made no movement. I then played the Surahs one after the other on the loudspeaker and began to listen, strenuously focusing on them. My jaw started to clench, as if someone was trying to break it, and my feet and arm began to turn. All of this was involuntary and petrifying. I lost consciousness.

Jan 18th, 2019

I repeated the procedure again today. It hurt a little less, but during the attempt, I saw a young girl with her back turned towards me, reciting something which did not sound like the Quran. When she turned towards me, I saw that it was seven–year–old me, and just then, my seven–year–old face started to disappear, melting off the bony structure. I have decided that I will go to the mosque tomorrow.

Jan 19th, 2019

I went to the mosque opposite my house. It took me forty minutes, since for every step that I took forward, I took two back. I thought that I would never make it, and I saw the dog from the rainy day weeks ago, growling and following me. I ran from it and made it to the *masjid.* I recall collapsing at the front door, and, like a weakling, following an *alima* inside a room. She said that I had a fever, and that she could sense that I was not alone. We later found out that a creature was clinging to my feet, not letting me walk.

Jan 20th, 2019

Today, the *alima* came to my house. Papa did not mind. He said that I could do any mumbo jumbo that I wanted as long as he did not have to pay for it. I do not remember what happened in today's session, but I feel better. I no longer want to see everyone naked. My headaches have increased.

Jan 21st, 2019

The *alima* says that I sing songs during the session. She *says* that till this process continues, I have to refrain from listening to music, reading Sidney Sheldon, and that I have to stay in *wudhu.* She says that it's not Radhika. It is an old man who does not walk on the ground, but on the air, and has been wanting to possess my body for years. She says that I need to be patient.

Jan 22nd, 2019

It is the third day today, and I feel light as a feather. The memory of the session is blurry, but the alima has assured me that the old man has left through my right arm. She *says* that years ago, I was singing songs in the park to my *maasi*, and it was not a Surah. She says that memory is an unreliable thing, and that *sheytaan* can manipulate us into Thinking the strangest things. She says that I should offer all my prayers. God will protect me with or without the necklace.

Chapter 12

The Boy who couldn't Jump

Sometimes – scratch that – quite often in life, we read a piece of writing, or hear a story, and without getting into the nitty gritty little details, we nod our heads in agreement. But you see, that's the thing about stories they have these dusty door handles from forty years ago and treasure chests under cellars, men whose pakora like Nubian noses mean something, and magenta colored curtains that reflect the mood of the wise old woman who is narrating those tales. So, read between the lines and decipher each alphabet slowly like you're drinking panadol syrup and be astonished if the lines decide to move.

On May 24th of the year 2001, when the weather in Lahore was balmy, and Mr. Azeem was often found comparing the heat under his wrinkled toes to his wife's flaming hot, peppery mutton dish on the stove, young Hussain came into the world. Each hour under the golden Lahori sun, Mr. Azeem complained about life testing his patience, his worn–out sandals, and the fact his son was born during the hottest months. Mrs. Azeem was partially unconscious, and because of the sudden heatwave, no relative had come to see the child. The hospital wanted the ward to be free for other summer children and Mr. Azeem found it hellish to carry a sobbing child and a wife who walked slower than the perspiration drops forming and dripping off his face, to his borrowed vehicle.

Mr. and Mrs. Azeem weren't bad parents; they just preferred loving their little one from a distance. Even though food supplies would run out ten days before the end of the month, the parents would somehow manage to pay the *maasi* to look after Hussain's needs. They liked showing off their son to relatives because Hussain was a happy child, bursting with energy and excitement. They also liked enrolling him into local newspaper advertisements. By age four, Hussain was already the face of a Gujarati pamper brand that later got banned for giving children fungal rashes, and had also appeared in the advertisement of an herbal teeth whitening medicine by a hakeem.

When Hussain turned seven and almost started going to school, someone suggested to Mr. Azeem that he should send Hussain to a cricket academy instead, because children who started off at an early age had a higher probability of being the next Afridi. Mr. Azeem already found cricket to be a game of respect and having done electrical engineering himself, he felt unhappy with the outcome. So, instead of memorizing his alphabets, Hussain was deciphering the ball and the bat with other baby players from the neighborhood. On the seventh day, the coach called in Mr. Azeem to tell him that his son did not know how to jump.

"He can walk, he can talk, he can run but he cannot jump. He just cannot lift himself off the ground." Mr. Azeem thought that it was a rather odd complaint.

"Of course, my son can jump. Teach him how." But the coach said that he just couldn't anymore.

"It's a basic thing, Azeem *Sahab. Koodo. Chalang lagao.* Jump. *Bacha nae kar pata hai."*

Complaining about the coach's useless teaching methodology, Mr. Azeem took Hussain home to teach him how to jump. He showed him videos of people jumping; Mr. and Mrs. Azeem jumped themselves – on the mattress, on the floor, on the freshly watered grass, and even on each other, but Hussain just stood still.

"Jump *beta*, Hussain." Mr. Azeem found himself pushing his child off the bed, which just led to his his wife frantically screaming at him because Hussain ended up breaking his front tooth. The parents installed a mini jumping castle the shape of Hussain's favorite cartoon Doraemon, which Mr. Azeem claimed to have picked off the shelf of Al–Fatah, but had in fact stolen from a shipment at a CNG station. Hussain would sit in the castle, roll in it, but could not, for whatever reason, jump on it. After four months of endless trying, Mr. and Mrs. Azeem gave up.

Theek hai. Koyi baat nahin. It's not like it's the end of his life. Doctor bane ga mera Hussain, Mr. Azeem thought.

The Azeems' nosy neighbor, Shagufta, who was studying to be a psychologist at BNU and lived alone – something Mr. Azeem highly disapproved of – suggested Mrs. Azeem take her son to a psychologist. She further explained the difference between a psychologist and a psychiatrist so that Mrs. Azeem was assured that nothing 'science–y' would go in her son's stomach. It would just be therapy. Mr. Azeem, who despised the thought of a woman liberated and living alone, frowned on her uncalled–for advice.

"Isay lagta hai hum apne betay say baat nahin karte? What foolishness. Now we have to pay a person who isn't even a doctor to talk to him?"

During that time, Hussain was shifted to his own bedroom because he would often wake up in the middle of the night and stare at what seemed to be his parents in their birthday suits on the TV screen. And then, traumatized by what he saw, wouldn't go back to sleep. Mr. Azeem would be adamant that his son had seen nothing, and Mrs. Azeem would lecture Hussain about how *agar bura scene aye, tou moun udher kar letay hain.* Mrs. Azeem brought an old bed from her parents' house to her son's room. Feeling an unusual longing for her son, she woke up early to put up Batman stickers on the bedroom wall, the ones the shopkeeper had given them with Hussain's new school shoes. The room was set, and the door closed on little Hussain, who sat staring at the Batman sticker in the middle of the *deemak* infested wall.

The next day, Mrs. Azeem opened the door to find Hussain lying on the shag yellow carpet. Hussain had not been able to jump onto the bed, so he had slept on the stained rug which he claimed smelt like the inside of baba's socks. Without any delay, Hussain was taken to a psychologist. His office was covered with framed certificates which assured Mrs. Azeem that the man could be the answer to correcting the ways of her problematic summer- born child.

Hussain enjoyed going to the psychologist. He learned that the doctor uncle's name was Hussain too, and after the weekly sessions, his baba would often buy him a kebab from the corner street shop. The moment Mrs. Azeem would prepare him to go to the 'good doctor *sahib*', Hussain would start salivating, Thinking about the treat awaiting him.

After three sessions and three kebabs, Mr. Hussain called in little Hussain's parents to discuss his analysis.

"There is good news and bad news. The good news is that whatever your son has, it is indeed psychological, which means that it can be cured. The bad news is that this mental disorder of his has grown over the years and will take time to resolve."

Mr. and Mrs. Azeem looked at each other. In that

moment, Mrs. Azeem felt like a huge burden had been lifted off her shoulders – knowing that her son would be able to jump like a normal human being. Mr. Azeem, on the other hand, had a lot of questions in his mind, none of which he bothered asking.

"Your son," the psychologist continued, "feels that every time he decides to jump, another version of him, made of fire, as he describes it, stops him. This thing he describes is human, and appears to be a doppelganger, and its feet are attached to Hussain's – only he's under the floor–on the other side, as told by your child."

Mr. Azeem frowned. "So, you mean to say that my son should not read Harry Potter? If that's your concern, you'll have to take it up with the LGS people, *bhai jaan.* They have those *sheytaani* books in their libraries."

"No," Mr. Hussain replied. *"Aisi baat nahin hai.* Your son has made an imaginary friend which he claims belongs to the other world. This friend is upside down, and its feet are attached to your son's. According to Hussain, he can only jump if his friend jumps."

"But my son never jumps–" Mrs. Azeem cut in, trying to make sense of what she was hearing.

"Ma'am, *wohi tou main apko keh raha houn.* All this is a fragment of his imagination. *Khayali pulao.* The moment he stops Thinking that there is a friend who stops him from jumping, he will start jumping."

There was an uncomfortable silence in the room, which

made Mr. Hussain believe that he should keep talking. "Now, I will keep on talking to Hussain to understand what has caused him to make this friend. Once we figure out the root cause, we will be able to diminish it with therapy."

"Acha tou mera beta pagal tou nahin hai na?"

"Nahin. Hum apke betay kou pagal hone nahin dain gay."

The truth was, which Mr. Hussain himself admitted to perhaps, although only in front of his bathroom mirror, that he did not know why little Hussain could not jump. But he had grown up solving the cheap Urdu Bazaar copy of the Rubik's cube, and so he felt that he could crack the code.

Little Hussain was not a peculiar child, but a rather ordinary boy with a peculiar problem. His therapy sessions continued for years only because Mrs. Azeem thought that if they stopped, her dear son would stop Thinking, eating, and even breathing. Just like he had stopped jumping after leaving her stomach.

Hussain grew up to become fascinated with funerals. When he was eight, his nana died. When he was ten, his *maasi* died and when he was twelve, his phupho died. Each time someone close to him died, he sneaked to check the lifeless body before it was bathed to see how different it would look after it was cleaned up. He thought that the art of preserving a body was utterly delightful and he told his father that he'd dress up people for funerals for a living. He later learned that he would be called a mortician and that his house would be a funeral house. The thought of all that gave him goosebumps – the kind he enjoyed. Mr. Azeem stopped taking interest in his son and decided to have another child who he planned to jump with the day he'd be born. Mrs. Azeem was instructed to plan in the late summer months so that the baby would come in the winter days and Mr. Azeem was definite that the baby would be a son, a mentally stable one.

After nine months, a daughter was born. She came out blue, not the shiny kind like Nestle Everyday milk sachets, but dull like a monsoon sky, and within four days, she perished. Hussain held her deceased tiny body in his hands and ran his bony fingers along her veins. He wanted to cut her up, fill her with fluids till her cheeks turned cherry red; he wanted to preserve her.

Two years later, a son was born. Mr. Azeem was delighted. The child looked nothing like Hussain, and wrapped in a woolen quilt with a huge forehead, he appeared to be a younger version of his father. In the evening, the newborn suddenly stopped crying, and his eyes drooped low–like a wilting *gulab* left unattended in a *baag*. By nighttime, he was no more. Hussain wanted to dress him in the finest silk and pin his eyes open so that his little brother could see the world for one last time.

After the second miscarriage, Mrs. Azeem had four more pregnancies, none of which ripened to bear her fruit, and during the last one, she died. Hussain wasn't allowed to bathe her, but he did instruct the woman doing so to put red lipstick on his ami's lips. He said that it was her favorite color. But since we're being honest here, Mrs. Azeem had never put on a dark shade in her life, for she thought she'd look too inviting. And yet, Hussain fantasized his ama in crimson red, the color of his night time *anaar.*

A *molvi* sitting next to the sobbing Mr. Azeem, who had hardly ever been affectionate towards his late wife, asked him if he believed in jinns.

"Jinns?"

"Yes, jinns," the *molvi* replied, "the misfortune that has fallen upon you is the work of jinns."

Mr. Azeem did not pay any heed to the talking man. It was a habit – not paying attention to things – or people. At night, he dreamt of his wife being dragged away by strong, broad- chested men with eyes on the backs of their heads.

A week later, on a December afternoon, Mr. Azeem stopped to have boiled eggs. *Garam* anday! *Garam* anday! The warmth of the soft yolk eased his mind. It was when he was done eating that he saw the *molvi* from the funeral standing next to him. Making small talk, he asked him what he had meant before. When the *molvi* stayed quiet, Mr. Azeem started talking about desi eggs and eggs in general.

The *molvi* smiled. "The son you have at home," he paused whilst chewing on his hard–boiled egg, "is the son of a jinn."

At that moment, out of all the nonsense that Mr. Azeem had heard over the years, he believed that the *molvi*'s sentence topped the list.

"Hear me out," the bearded man spoke, standing under the shade of a *banyan* tree. "Your wife bore no children. It was not because she couldn't; it was because her womb wasn't welcoming. The boy you call your son is, in fact, the brother of a jinn. Years ago, when you would engage in lovemaking without *dua*, and stay in the same condition of *na–paaki,* my elder brother attached himself to your wife. But, only for the night. He enjoyed what you enjoyed. And when Hussain was born, so was Kamran– but in an alternate world. The truth is that he's always been with Hussain. Inseparable. And your son's nature isn't that of humans, and over time, he has learned that."

Disturbed, but intrigued, Mr. Azeem turned around to get his plate of eggs. When he turned back, the *molvi* had disappeared into thin air. Just like that – in the blink of an eye, like the switching of a tv channel, the flipping of a *tandoori roti,* and the sudden change in weather when holding a summer- born boy.

"Kya Azeem chacha. *Khare khare kis say baatein kar rahein hain. Anday khaein."*

Mr. Azeem placed the egg in his mouth, and with a shiver running down his spine, asked the boy selling eggs where the *molvi* who had just been buying from him had gone.

"Konsa molvi? Subah say bus apne mujh say anday khareedain hain."

Chapter 13

Odd Stories from the streets of Pakistan

There was once a scientist residing in the streets of Istanbul who tested his liquid creation with a litmus paper. Instead of turning a color given on the chart, the paper turned sparkly golden, and then when dipped again, the white of the galaxies appeared, and when dipped the third time, the litmus paper turned thin and delicate – like the petal of an autumn flower. The Turkish scientist drank the mysterious liquid, wrote about his findings in a journal, and disappeared from a room that was locked from outside.

Now, this tale might seem inexplicable since there are little details to it. But a story that was unexplainable to the wisest men then is still strange now. Some said that the scientist was a jinn, others said that the potion he had created made him a jinn, and, well, the newspaper wrote that the Americans had kidnapped him because his discovery had been nuclear – *oh*, the endless possibilities.

Today, we have such troubling tales that have happened in houses, *masjids,* and even *shaadi* halls. And though there is much truth to it, there is little the mind can understand.

Abida Shameem slept till noon every day for years after her wedding. She was a good wife, and a rather caring *bahu,* but whatever she did or took care of had to be done once the afternoon set in. *Nashta*s had to be missed, and when her bhabhi had a son at 6 am, she wasn't there to congratulate her because well, everyone knew that Shameem slept till noon. This hadn't always been the case. As a young bride, Shameem had been up making breakfast for her husband and pressing his shirts after, but it all changed one morning.

Shameem had been frying eggs – without yolk, like her husband preferred them – and her husband had come in, and for the very first time, helped her make his breakfast. Astonished and happy, she had then set the eggs and orange juice on the table and called to her husband, who had gone to wash his hands, but had found him still in his night suit and nightcap, snoring in bed. Upon waking up, he hadn't recalled helping her. The next day, her husband came into the kitchen again and this time, brushed Shameem's curls off her forehead, softly *ki*sssing her.

He said that the sun made her look beautiful and that he was lucky to have her. A minute later, Shameem went inside and saw her husband sitting on the couch, sipping tea. Startled, she saw that in front of her sat her grumpy husband, and out in the kitchen stood her husband, smiling at her with a twinkle in his eyes signaling her to step out again. For the entirety of the next week, she would often see her husband in two places, and the one who couldn't step outside the kitchen was her 'morning husband', who came and went with the sun. He cherished her, massaged her feet, and even had an egg with the yolk. But of course, the more she saw her morning husband, the less attracted she felt towards her real one and soon, she found herself falling out of love with the man she had married for all mornings, noons, and nights. It was then that Shameem decided that she would sleep till noon, for she was a loyal woman with good morals. She never saw her morning husband again.

Mumtaz Khan met an elderly woman during her Fajar prayers once. She lived in a far–off town, where the women, too, had a *masjid* they could go to five times a day. Mumtaz talked out her problems while worshipping God, and then with the women around her, and her life felt happening. The elderly woman that she met was her mother's age and could hardly kneel and pray, but she had come to seek forgiveness and find her creator.

While Mumtaz and the other woman would leave, the elderly woman stayed there as if it was her home, and wept till her eyes could produce no more tears. There were rumors that she had created a rift between her son and his wife, and so her son had left her. She called onto God to bring him back. But of course, Mumtaz didn't believe them. She knew that after the *jayanemaaz* was folded, the women came back to their womanly senses and talked the devil's talk.

Soon, a machine could be seen in the corner of the prayer room. It was to help the elderly woman breathe. The management said that the woman had always had difficulty breathing, and since she spent most of her time with God, it was their duty to help her with the worldly matters. One day, out of curiosity, Mumtaz asked the elderly woman why she sobbed so much, and if it was because of her long–lost son.

"No," the woman replied in between cries, "I cannot breathe, and I do not have a problem. Someone presses my throat till I collapse, and no medication can treat it. I'm here to ask God to cure it."

Mumtaz looked at her wrinkling face. "Was this problem always there?" The woman looked up and pressed her lips together, as if to taste the tears. "You don't have to answer if you don't want to," Mumtaz added, feeling like one of those women who ask too many questions.

"No, I started having it when I started killing people. You see, I worked as a nurse in the ICU unit, and someone from the family, never the mothers, would pay me to take off their oxygen mask so that their artificial breathing would stop. I would do just that. I thought I was helping them by taking their breath, and now they're taking mine."

The television in Mr. and Mrs. Farooq's house stopped working the day Mrs. Farooq got pregnant with their second daughter, Momina. Over the next few months, the blender stopped blending smoothies, and the electric heater refused to turn on no matter how many times it got repaired. One day, when Mrs. Farooq wasn't home, their neighbor requested the house help to lend her Mrs. Farooq's blender. Not knowing about the faulty machine, she handed it over. At night, Mrs. Farooq received a thank you call about how her blender had been a lifesaver. Other incidents followed that made the couple realize that the electrical appliances didn't work in *their house,* but worked outside.

So, the plugs were inspected, and the wires were altered. On one occasion, when Mrs. Farooq was at her mother's place, Mr. Farooq informed her that they no longer needed to go television shopping, because the HD screen had miraculously started working. But, when Mrs. Farooq excitedly reached home to watch the last episode of *Humsafar,* the television channels started changing on their own.

"There is some static energy that is interrupting all the appliances in the house," the inspection team told the couple. "It's odd because it usually happens near nuclear plants and other such stations with electromagnetic activity."

The problem reached a point where Mr. Farooq started looking for houses in other societies and even cities. "It was bearable in the winter, but how will we sleep without fans?" he asked his wife.

A house in the corner of the street they lived in was finalized, and they decided to move right after Momina's birth. Momina came out looking just like Mrs. Farooq's mother, with a snout nose the size of a peanut, and lips the color of an old Crayola crayon. She was a delicate thing and too delicate to be born in a dark room, with a heartbeat that could not be monitored.

The doctors thought that she was going to die, not because she was a feeble thing, but because there was no light, and all the machines were malfunctioning.

"It's Satan's doing," a nurse was heard whispering. "Something bad is going to happen." But nothing bad happened. Momina was wrapped in a quilt that looked pink but was indeed green – something that Mrs. Farooq noticed in the sunlight. She was taken home where, again, there was no electricity.

Within some months, the couple realized that it wasn't their house, it was their *daughter*. When she had been in the stomach, the appliances had gone off, and now that she was out, nothing around her worked – not even their mobile phones. When they drove around the streets of Faisalabad, the glass in the lamp posts shattered one by one. When they attended *shaadi*s, all the photos came out blank and blurry.

And when Momina wept, the voltage buzzed out of the house's sockets. Today, their first daughter stays with her chacha, and Mr. and Mrs. Farooq have moved to an isolated place in Karachi located behind a private beach. Momina is learning how to harvest her aura and this ability that she possesses, and her parents are leading a happy life without electricity.

Suleman Feroz was a poor man. His father sold samosas in old Lahore, and they were crispy treats that many enjoyed with the rain. There was a specific way to boil the potatoes and mash them, and an even more specific way to add the salt and the spices before placing them in the flour bed. According to Feroz, Suleman's father–this classified information was what made the savory delights the best in the market.

There was a complete art to it. Suleman, who could see the trickling sweat fall from his father's forehead into the batter, looked away in disgust. "I don't want to sell samosas," he said. And Suleman didn't. When he turned eighteen, he ran away with a few stolen rupees smudged with his abu's oily fingerprints from frying crusts all night long.

Days of starvation made Suleman settle for a caretaking job at a graveyard in a town near Multan. The job was simple, he had to count the graves before sleeping and then clean them in the morning. He had seen horror shows growing up when their khala's television worked, and all of them showed haunted graves and walking corpses.

But, nothing like that actually happened. Sure, there were occasional *qissay* that Suleman was told, about women and men being caught doing *kaala jadoo,* and teenagers who snuck in, trying to complete dares, but that was it. There were no jinns and headless men. One night, whilst guarding the graves at the back, Suleman heard a rather odd voice. At first, he assumed that some kids had broken in, trying to film the *kabrain,* and he ran out with a stick in an attempt to shoo them away. But, as he stepped outside, he realized that the voice, which now sounded like a cry, was coming from underneath the ground.

"Who, who is it?" Suleman gulped, trying to hide the fear in his voice. *"Koun hai?"* With his *guneghar,* father–leaving eyes, he saw that the grave was moving – akin to how a person moves under a blanket, wriggling, trying to get free. Suleman dug the grave a little with the stick, mostly with his hands, till the dirt no longer settled in his nails. The mud unfolded to reveal a sitting corpse, covered with blazing red serpents which no human had ever seen. The hairless body, with skin a shade of pale blue extended his greasy hand and placed it on Suleman's leg. Its eyes turned upward. "Samosa *khao gay?*" it said with a toothless grin.

Pimples and zits – we've all had them at one time or the other. Rotten things – forever ruining our beauty – just like the powerful *zameendar* who take possession of a place that is not theirs – our faces. Some are red, the color of a three–day old pomegranate, and some yellow–like the food coloring of biryani. Others ooze white, a satisfaction that leads to scarring. Oh, the misery.

Saniya had never gotten a pimple in her life, and her husband had flawless tan skin, so smooth that you could slide right off it. They were a family free of acne. Their six year old daughter, Rushna, woke up screaming one day – as spoiled as she was – demanding them to get rid of the big zit on her cheek. It was purple like a bruised peach, and was standing tall with confidence, like a small man–made Islamabadi hill. Initially, they calmed her with a breakfast of Koko Crunch, and told her that it would go away on its own.

However, it seemed to grow overnight, and on top of that pimple, another one appeared – like aunty Rafiqa's gray cushion throw on her very gray cushions too light to be seen, but when closely inspected, could be spotted. This time, no cereal could calm Rushna down. She refused to go to school, and threatened to kill herself. Had Saniya been my mother,

I would have gotten a tight slap across the face, but it was the maid who got that, for Saniya felt that her unclean hands had caused her daughter to break out.

When her husband returned, they rushed her to their family doctor, who brushed off their concerns by claiming that it was, in fact, nothing serious. On the third day, the horror began. Rushna reported that the pimple was alive under the skin and when told to describe it, she said, "It's like it's an earthworm, baba, which has mistaken my skin for rain."

Specialist after specialist, they roamed the cities, and with ointments, injections and assuring promises, returning home only to find the pimple larger than before, now covering half their daughter's face. And now, rather than treating it, the doctors had started getting amused by it.

"I have a friend in Qatar," Saniya told her husband, "Mama's friend. She says that it's best to get her checked there. I was instructed to book a dermatologist on Meddy online, and she'll take it from there." So, they flew to Qatar, with all their savings and the hopes of getting their daughter the best doctor. It went fairly well. A cyst was removed, and the infection was eliminated. Other than pink lining around the cut and a stitch, Rushna's face looked normal.

Satisfied, they went back home. The X–rays confirmed that the issue had indeed been addressed. But like an unpredictable storm, and a bad fall in your new *dawat* clothes, Rushna's dissolved stitch got covered with small threads popping from within her skin, like a grapevine attached to the house's wall, a year after the procedure.

"We don't have any money,' Saniya sighed. "We can't go back to Qatar." The hole, now open, excreted sticky green liquid, and the odor of dead fish.

"If the qualified doctors on Meddy couldn't cure it," a skin specialist from Karachi said, "we are clueless." But that wasn't the alarming part – Rushna said that her pimple whispered to her, told her to cut her mother's hair and burn her father's files. And then one day, Saniya caught her daughter giggling because her pimple had told her a bad joke.

"It's saying that baba's business trips aren't really business trips, mama." Horrified, Rushna's mother took her to a psychiatrist. Multiple sittings later, the parents were told that the recurrence of the disease had impacted Rushna's cognitive abilities. One evening, however, when Saniya bent down to change the bandage on her daughter's cheek, she herself heard something whispering her name. A non–believer of ghosts and magic, Saniya ended up rushing her daughter to a local *molvi*.

"I have told you exactly what has happened till now," she begged. "There's something mysterious happening. I need your help." The elderly man looked at the preteen and bit his lip. He pretended to talk to someone, and then told Rushna to apologize to thin air. "Your daughter made fun of a girl at school a year ago. She had acne–prone skin. What your daughter didn't know was that she came from a family where jinns were passed as family presents for generations. She ended up offending something that was with that girl. The jinn pecked your daughter on the cheek, and since then, your daughter has been suffering from a curse. It's alright though – the apology has been made."

Printed in the USA
CPSIA information can be obtained
at www.ICGtesting.com
LVHW092349200624
783629LV00034B/992
9 789698 729240